SIMON SAYS

Provoke Chuck Simon, the Complex told mob boss Tony. Push him. See if his power will manifest.

Tony had pushed, all right. And the power had manifested into the hideous deaths of six men.

Now, Chuck advanced on Tony, saying, "Simon says stand."

Pure mental force yanked Tony to his feet.

"Simon says die."

An invisible fist grabbed Tony and squeezed, collapsing his heart and lungs. Brain oozed out of his ears . . .

PSI-MAN

Mind-Force Warrior

PSI-MAN

DAVID PETERS

CHARTER/DIAMOND BOOKS, NEW YORK

PSI-MAN

A Charter/Diamond Book/published by arrangement with
the author

PRINTING HISTORY
Charter/Diamond edition/October 1990

ISBN: 1-55773-399-6

PRINTED IN THE UNITED STATES OF AMERICA

10 9 8 7 6 5 4 3 2 1

October 12, 2021

1

THEY CAUGHT UP with him in Kansas.

Not that he knew that he had been caught up with. Hardly that. To him, Kansas, and this particular town in Kansas by the name of Taylor's Point, was not much different from any of the previous towns the circus had passed through.

Their stay at Taylor's Point had begun as innocuously as in the other cities. Innocuously, that is, for the employees and inhabitants of the Four Star Carnival and Circus. For them it was old hat. For the inhabitants of Taylor's Point, it was nothing short of miraculous.

Four Star's series of trucks, trailers, and transports had wended its way down the interstate from its previous gig in LaPoint. It was a dazzling assortment of vehicles in various states of disrepair. The best-working truck had a muffler with a hole the size of Sacramento. There weren't all that many animals: a couple of lions past their prime, a fairly small elephant, a couple of horses.

It was as if the circus itself was almost an afterthought, which it was. The main source of revenue was the countless skill booths and the handful of rides, all neatly collapsible and transportable. Four Star was a rolling

testament to the American dream of cheesy family enter-
tainment.

All of the support personnel rode in a handful of Win-
nebagos. The hours of their transport were long and gray,
staring out at endless stretches of wheat fields and the like
that suggested an innocuous, innocent American spirit that
had long since been ruthlessly stomped away.

Chuck stared out the window, his eyes locked on the
skies. He rolled slightly back and forth, swaying to the
gentle motion of the van, staring upward. From behind
him, further back in the van, there was the familiar smack-
ing sound of pasteboard on pasteboard, plastic chips being
tossed, and potato chips being crunched. The ongoing,
ever-continuous card game was in progress.

Chuck's square jaw rested on his hands as he stared
toward the horizon. Apparently in his late twenties, he was
a disarmingly handsome man. His hair was jet black, as
was the thick beard he had grown in recent months. Originally his hair had been blonde, but his beard always grew
in very dark and he had taken advantage of that by dyeing
his hair to match. Anything to disguise his appearance.

He had snapping blue eyes that women found endlessly
fascinating. His nose was slightly irregular, the gift of a
profound breaking while playing college football. He had
high cheekbones and neatly placed dimples when he
smiled.

His forehead was fairly high, but it wasn't as if his hair
were receding. He'd always had that vast expanse of forehead. When he was a kid, the other kids said he looked
dorky. His mother said he looked scholarly. When he'd
grown up his mother's opinion had seemed to be the right
one, although the occasional smart ass still looked into
Chuck's shiny forehead and smoothed their own hair as if
consulting a mirror. Chuck would grin lopsidedly and bear

such foolishness. It did him no harm. "Kept him honest," as his father always said.

From behind him a voice called, "Jesus God, Chuck, what's the big fascination?"

He knew the voice as Paul's without turning around. "With what?" he asked.

"Outside. You always stare outside for hours when we travel, like you're waiting for a sign or something."

The pasteboard slapping had sped up a little. That meant Dakota was dealing.

"No sign," said Chuck evenly. "Maybe just a break in the sky."

"Forget it," Dakota's lilting voice now came as the dealing ceased. "Forecast for today is gray, followed by rain. Like yesterday. Like the day before. Like always."

Chuck turned away and walked slowly over toward the card players. He settled next to Dakota. Chuck got along with everyone. It was his specialty. But Dakota he had a special fondness for.

She studied her cards but shot a quick, friendly glance in his direction. "So the great outcast finally deigns to sit with us lowly card players," she said.

He grinned. "Is that what I am?"

Dexter, bespectacled and lean, cautious to the point of distraction, methodically rearranged his hand as was his ritual. "You never play cards with us," he said through his nose.

"Man's right," said Harry, who rounded out the foursome. In contrast to the slim Paul seated next to him, Harry was bulky and muscular. He worked out with weights constantly, determined not to let the muscles he'd built up in his youth become flabby and unpleasant. Harry was also the lion tamer for the circus, although that job held a minimum of danger. The idea that the lions had any predisposition to attack Harry was ludicrous. Their main concern was where their next meal was coming from, and the answer to that was, quite simply, from Harry. They knew that. So to kill the meal ticket would be absurd.

Chuck got a little closer to Dakota. She was a compactly built woman, with long brown hair that she was wearing up in a chignon. Her t-shirt hung perpetually off one shoulder and her jeans were carefully ripped at the knees. Since Chuck had joined Four Star a month back, there had been an innocent teasing relationship between the two. Chuck knew that Dakota wouldn't mind in the least if it went further than that. In truth, neither would he. But a relationship, particularly physical, was something he took quite seriously, and was not something he would consider entering into transiently.

Right now, most of his life was transient.

A month was the longest he'd spent with any one group in quite some time. He wondered how much longer it would last.

"I don't play cards, Dex," said Chuck evenly, "since I'd hate to take your money. Wouldn't be fair."

"Ooohhh," said Paul in a loud, semi-mocking voice. "Not fair! Well, damn nice of you watching out for us like that."

"No problem," smiled Chuck. He glanced at Dakota's cards. She dropped two and replaced them with enough to give her two pair, jacks over tens.

He shifted his gaze to the stacks of chips as the game proceeded briskly. Within moments Paul and Dex had dropped out, and Harry and Dakota were staring at each other over the tops of their cards. Now Chuck's gaze flickered from one to the other.

Like a serene Buddha, Harry flipped two more chips in. "See your five and raise another five."

Dakota looked in annoyance at her almost non-existent pile. "Crap, Harry, you know that's more than I got. I can't see the bet."

"I'll take something in trade."

There were snickers from Dexter and Paul.

"Yeah," said Dakota, "I'll bet you would."

"Would you bet?" he asked, a rakish smile on his face. "Now that is the question. How much is a night with you worth, Dakota?"

"More'n you've got," she replied. There was no heat in the response. They knew each other too well for that. Harry had simply been trying to nail Dakota for months. An honorable goal that she could respect. She wasn't all that interested in him, but then again she wasn't all that disinterested. It was a question of just how far she was willing to go for a poker hand.

"Well, I'm betting more'n you've got, so we can call it even."

She tried to get a reading from his face, but there was no sign of expression. That usually meant that he held a pretty good hand . . . indeed, that's why Dex and Paul had folded. When Harry had a lousy hand you could usually tell. The whimpering was a tip off, for one thing.

The Winnebago rocked slightly under them as it hit a patch of unpaved road. Dakota looked challengingly at Chuck. "Think he's bluffing? Think I can beat him?"

"You really want to know?" replied Chuck.

The question was so calm that she blinked slightly at it. "Yeah, sure. Really."

"He's bluffing. You can beat him."

"Oh really?" Harry said, his eyes peering over the tops of his cards. "What am I holding?"

"Garbage," said Chuck.

Dakota looked from one to the other. There was no

trace of uncertainty in Chuck's face at all. Surely it was a guess on his part, but he didn't act like it. "You sure?"

"Always."

"Got a lot riding on this, Chuck," she said. "My virtue is at stake here."

"Penny ante bet," suggested Paul.

She ignored him. "So you sure?" she asked again.

"Always." Just the same way as before, exact same tone, as if he were talking from another country.

"Okay," she said, and "Okay," again as if to reassure herself. "Call. What've you got, Harry?"

"Full house, kings over jacks," he said.

She closed her eyes in pain.

Dex glanced over at Harry's hand. "Bullshit," he said. "You've got garbage."

Paul snickered.

"Thanks, genius," said Harry.

"Garbage? Really?" said Dakota.

"Yeah, garbage, okay? Happy? Saaa-tiss-fied?" He tossed down the cards. "Busted flush. Okay? Thanks a lot, Chuck," he snapped.

"What did I do?"

"I work for two weeks on my poker face and you friggin' tell her I've got garbage."

"You did."

"Who asked you?"

"She did."

"And how did you know?"

He smiled. "I did."

"Great."

"Would you like me to play a hand?"

"No, but I wouldn't mind backing the van over you."

And from behind them came a low growl.

Chuck's glance briefly flickered in its direction. "Quiet, Rommel," he said. "Harry was just kidding."

Harry turned and gasped and jumped, knocking over the chips. "Jesus God! That monster's in the van!"

"Rommel goes where I go," said Chuck calmly.

"Good. When you go to hell, take him with you."

Dakota hooted at that. "Some wild animal trainer. Afraid of a doggy."

Rommel padded forward from the shadows where he'd been lying with preternatural quiet. He was big for a German shepherd. He was big for a horse, which is what he really seemed like, and it was nothing short of astounding that he'd been able to lie there all that time and attract no attention at all. His fur was light brown, except for a large black spot on his back and a zigzag pattern on his forehead that had earned him his name.

"That's not a doggy," said Harry, shifting around so that his back was no longer to Rommel. "I've driven smaller cars than that thing. That thing would scare my lions."

"So would a Girl Scout troop," said Dakota.

The Girl Scout reared back and threw.

The ball fell short of the cans and ricocheted harmlessly away.

Chuck smiled sympathetically. All around him now was the invigorating hustle and bustle of the carnival. This was what had attracted him to this lifestyle. The carnival had a perpetual small-time innocence about it, something that reminded him of what he had given up and yet held out a hope for him, however vague, that somehow he might be able to recapture it.

He was surrounded by the familiar sounds, the shills trying to tempt men to display their machismo for the little

ladies by purchasing three throws for a dollar and winning
a worthless stuffed toy. The distant music of the calliope,
recorded and piped through speakers since the real calliope had broken months before Chuck even joined Four
Star. The constant hum and chatter of customers, of babies
crying mixed with the squeaking of pushed strollers. The
sound of popping corn and the aroma of hot pretzels.

None of which mattered worth a damn to the Girl Scout
who had had her eye on the pink poodle in the upper left
hand corner and had been determined to win it. The little
blonde girl stood there as if she'd lost her best friend. "I
came so close," she said, voice laced with misery.

Chuck, from behind the counter, nodded sympathetically. "I thought so too," he said. "Want to try again?
Only three for a dollar. Knock down the cans, win a—"

But the Girl Scout's mother, lips pursed severely, was
having none of it. "I told you it was a waste of money,"
she said, as if her daughter's failure was a personal triumph. "Now come on."

"Please Mommy . . ." She held up her card. "I'll put
it on my card . . ."

"No. We set a limit on how much you'd be allowed.
You're at it now."

"But Mommmmmmeeeee . . ." She seemed to be vi-
brating in place.

Unseen at Chuck's feet, Rommel rumbled disapprov-
ingly. The girl's high-pitched whining was getting on his
nerves.

"Tell you what," said Chuck, holding the balls out.
"Three throws. If you hit it, it's free, plus you win," and
he gestured, "one of these nifty prizes."

The mother stared at Chuck thoughtfully and decided
that if her daughter missed she would stalk off in high

dudgeon, claiming it was fixed and she shouldn't have to pay.

Chuck knew damned well that's what she was thinking. It didn't matter.

The mother nodded curtly, and the little girl took the offered balls. She bit her lower lip, aimed, and then reared back and threw the first one.

The trajectory looked like it was off by a good two feet, but then the ball suddenly veered towards the cans and smacked into them, sending them crashing resoundingly to the floor.

The mother looked stunned as the girl clapped her hands in delight.

"Whoa!" said Chuck. "That is one nasty curve!" Even as he spoke he started to reach for the stuffed pink poodle, but then he checked the gesture. "Which one would you like?"

"The pink poodle, please," she said carefully, as if saying the wrong thing would shatter the magic moment.

He nodded as he pulled the poodle down and handed it to her. She clutched at it lovingly and her mother, more out of reflex than any need for courtesy, said, "Say thank you."

"Thank you," the girl said.

He nodded and tossed off a salute as they walked away. Rommel looked up gratefully. *Thank you.*

"Welcome," said Chuck.

"What is it with you?"

Chuck turned in response to that last statement, which had been issued by the portly owner who was waddling over toward him. His name was Gwynn, and from his overall demeanor he was generally referred to as Penguin, although never to his face.

Next to him was Dakota, now decked out in a brief,

spangled costume that she wore for her tightrope act. Dakota could frequently be found near him. She knew which side her bread was buttered on.

"With me, Mr. Gwynn?"

"You give away more prizes than any two barkers here."

He shrugged expansively. "The people win, sir. That little girl knocked over the cans. What was I supposed to do?"

"I don't know! Chat it up when they throw. Distract them. Do *something*. All I know is that people come up to this booth and nine times out of ten, they turn into Dwight Gooden. They—oh, shit."

"What?" said Dakota.

"Cutters."

His gaze had traveled in the direction of three people, men whose clothes were tattered and whose general appearance and demeanor was of not caring about personal hygiene, or much else for that matter. They were wandering slowly through the carnival, looking about as if what they were seeing wasn't really there.

"How did those cardless wonders get in here?" he demanded. Chuck shrugged, as did Dakota. Gwynn waddled off, fists balled, determined to get them the hell out of his carnival.

Dakota and Chuck watched him go with amusement. "He hates non-paying customers," said Chuck.

"It's not just that," said Dakota. "Sometimes the police show up and roust the cutters, and that always makes a big scene. Who needs that kind of grief. By the way," and she was looking at the top of Chuck's chest, which was exposed by the open top buttons of his flannel shirt. "What's with the 'A'?"

"What?"

She pointed and he looked down. He'd almost forgotten he was wearing it.

"On that chain around your neck," she said. "That weird, metal letter 'A' bent out of a spoon. But your name is Chuck. What's you last name?"

"It doesn't start with 'A', if that's what you mean."

"Okay, so what does the 'A' stand for?"

" 'Always,' as in always thinking of you."

She moaned. "Oh God, Chuck, don't be like the rest of them. Don't turn into a sweet-talking asshole."

"Maybe that's what the 'A' stands for."

"Maybe you're right," and she tossed off a grin as she walked away.

He smiled goofily off at her and looked down at Rommel. Rommel looked up at him blandly. *Asshole.*

"Well, who asked you?"

Now there was no sign of the cutters or Gwynn. He must have successfully convinced them to leave without—

Without—

Chuck froze.

It was as if the air around him had suddenly changed, filled with electricity.

From at his feet there came a growl. Rommel was crouching now, hair raising on the nape of his neck. It was doing the same on Chuck's.

Them.

"I know," said Chuck in a low voice. "Where from?"

Can't tell.

"Me neither." It was a feeling he hated. Knowing that somewhere there was danger, but not being able to detect the origin.

He scanned the crowd quickly. The demeanor of his surroundings had changed completely. Suddenly the most innocent looking of families became a clever ploy. A carriage no longer contained an unseen baby, but a machine gun. And that priest over there was acting pretty damned suspiciously. . . .

Calm down.

"Shut up, Rommel. I'm fine."

You're not fine. Your mind is screaming and I'm getting a headache. I'll find them and kill them and—

"No," he hissed. "No killing."

What do you expect me to do? Charm them with my wit?

Chuck did not respond. He swung his legs over the top of the counter and stood in front of it. His hands were slightly out to his sides, as if he was balancing himself on an invisible tightrope.

People were now hurrying past him. The circus part of the carnival was under way, and since admission to that was part of the ticket, no one wanted to miss it.

"They aren't sure we're here."

I know.

"But how did they get the notion that we were?"

Well, they didn't hear it from me.

He reached out with his mind, trying to sweep the crowd. He was buffeted by emotions, trying to sort out a single sound from a maelstrom, one note from a concerto.

He spun. Rommel was heading towards the circus tent.

"Where are you going?" he shouted.

Where do you think?

The tent. They were in the tent. Rommel had homed in on them before he had. Chuck excelled at subtleties and shadings of human emotion, but when it came to tracking thoughts of violence, Rommel always had the upper hand.

Paw. Whatever.

And Rommel would not hesitate, upon finding them, to rip their throats out on Chuck's behalf.

He darted after Rommel, threading his way through the rapidly thickening crowd. His pulse was pounding against his temple and he lurched slightly as he tried to send out feelers. Now he had detected them as well, the freefloating tendency towards violence, combined with the suspicion that Chuck was somewhere nearby.

He should have just turned and gotten the hell out of the place. The moment that he had realized he'd been found out, he should have put as much distance between himself and the carnival as possible.

Rommel, however, was not predisposed to running. He was ready to kill something.

He lost visual track of Rommel but sensed him ahead somewhere. He couldn't be gentle anymore, and as the crowd thickened ahead of him, he started shoving with more than his hands. People suddenly staggered and glowered at each other, thinking that someone next to them had shoved them. Chuck, meantime, ran through them and into the circus tent.

The opening clowns had just finished their routine as Chuck reached the outskirts of the single ring. He didn't run into it, obviously. Might as well just send up a red flag. Instead he dropped back, hugging the perimeter, walking slowly around the grandstands and trying to get a feel for where his pursuers (Pursuers? Yes, yes, there was definitely more than one. He was certain of it) were hiding.

Hiding. They were sitting out in the open, he realized. He was the one skulking under the grandstands.

What had he come to?

In the ring they had rolled out the lions' cage. Chuck heard Harry's prerecorded theme music bellow over the tent speakers, the familiar sound of the whip cracking as Harry entered the cage. The three lions roared a greeting, but really it was nothing more than that. The lions and Harry knew the drill.

Slowly, carefully, he stalked the stalkers.

Seconds crawled by as he sifted through the barrage of minds that crossed his. Like two thoughts, passing in the night. . . .

His entire body was cloaked in sweat. Where the hell were they? Where was Rommel? Where—

And then the lions roared.

Really roared.

Chuck froze in his tracks, and there was a collective gasp from the crowd. Something had changed, something new had entered the lion tamer/lion relationship. Something very huge and very ugly, and Chuck wasn't sure what it was, but he was sure that someone might get killed over it. That someone being Harry.

He darted out through an opening in the grandstands just in time to hear the shrieking begin.

In the center of the ring, in the big cat cage, Harry was under siege.

He had backed against the far edge of the cage, escape blocked by the lions. Their calm, placid demeanor that occasionally bored audiences to tears, had vanished. It had been replaced by a wild, berserk fury that had caught their trainer and friend completely off guard.

The ringmaster had frozen, uncertain of what to do. Roustabouts were running about, grabbing up long sticks to try and shove through the cage to push the lions away from Harry. The crowd was rumbling in confusion. Perhaps, they were thinking, this was part of the act, but if it was it was a damned unpleasant part. The first stirrings of panic were beginning to blossom forth.

Chuck reached out into Harry's mind, trying to get a sense of what was happening. There was nothing. Harry was as confused as anyone, but in considerably more danger.

Harry tried to edge around toward the door at the far end, but the stalking lions would have none of it. They converged on Harry and just as Chuck got there, the first one leaped.

The crowd started to scream, for now they knew, really knew, that something had gone hideously, fatally wrong. Chuck staggered slightly, buffeted by the mass hysteria, and he slammed shut his psychic blocks even as he grabbed at the door of the cage. Harry went down beneath the weight of the first lion, and he howled in terror and agony. The lion's fetid breath washed over him, the roar alone threatening to crush his skull.

The door was locked. Harry had the key.

Chuck, forcing panic from his mind, reached into the lock with his mind. He felt the outline of the tumblers, made a gentle push, and they clicked. He yanked the door open and leaped in.

One of the lions turned immediately. And Chuck, without taking the time to think of what he was doing, reacted instinctively to protect the crowd. He slammed the door behind himself, locking himself in with Harry and the lions so that the great beasts couldn't escape.

"Stop," Chuck told the lion firmly.

The lion, not six paces away, roared and leaped at Chuck.

Chuck's hands seemed to blur, and suddenly the lion was slammed up against the other side of the cage. Chuck spun away, keeping his back to the cage the entire time. The lion tracked him, its great head never moving, and it leaped again.

This time there was no room to maneuver and Chuck

did the only thing he could. He lashed out with the pure force of his mind.

The TK blast hurled the lion back, and Chuck screamed as a bolt of agony backlashed through his head. He felt warm fluid pouring from his nostrils and knew that his nose was bleeding. He'd overexerted himself. But what choice did he have?

The confused lion was trying to pull itself together as Chuck darted toward the other two. Harry was shrieking under them and Chuck grabbed them by their tails and yanked with all his strength, augmented by the power of his mind. The lions were drawn back from Harry, roaring their fury.

Now roustabouts were at the cage, shoving with their sticks that had rounded hoops at the edges, hoping to snag some of the beasts' heads to hold them back. All three lions were now converging on Chuck.

He leaped. Straight up.

His hands snagged the crossbars that were a good ten feet off the ground. He swung his leg up, yelling as a swipe of a lion's paw just managed to rake across his thigh. An inch closer and it would have laid open the skin to the bone.

The lions stalked beneath him, trying to leap up at him. Every time they did he mentally shoved them back down again, keeping them at bay. His nose had turned into a goddamn geyser. He couldn't move. His full concentration was keeping the lions from leaping up at him. He couldn't even spare a portion of his mind to think of crawling forward on the bars, and besides, where the hell was he going to go?

Somewhere Gwynn was shouting "Tranks! Get the trank guns!"

And another animal snarl was in the cage.

Rommel had miraculously squeezed his great frame through the bars and now, fearlessly, insanely, he leaped into the lions, scattering them.

For one moment the lions stalked, confused about the newcomer. Rommel stood his ground, growling his defiance. Chuck, in his link with Rommel, sensed the dog's communication with the lions, and he sensed that it was not going well.

Quickly Chuck swung his legs down and dropped to the ground. He darted over towards Harry's mauled body and, at that moment, the lions attacked.

Without a second's hesitation Rommel threw himself between Chuck and the lions. His growls matched the lions' own, and he snapped fiercely at them, going for their vulnerable bellies, moving quickly to avoid the swipes of their paws and the hideous snapping of their teeth.

Harry was slumped against the bars, barely breathing.

The door was still at the far end, the mass of fighting animals' bodies making it seem a mile off. From all around him people were shouting. Everything was complete chaos.

Chuck reached into himself, found a calm center, and grabbed the bars.

He pulled at them for show, because an adrenalin rush might make what happened next believable.

The bars bent.

Chuck shuddered, a gray fog rolling in on him, and he fought it back. Within seconds he had opened the bars enough that Harry's unmoving body was shoved through into the eager, unquestioning hands of the other workers. Chuck hurled himself through, then spun, slamming his hand on the ground.

"Rommel! Come on!"

Rommel leaped above the claws of one of the lions and dashed towards the opening. Before he had squeezed through, but now he had no time. He would have to get through in an instant.

The lions, with a deafening roar, leaped after him, and Rommel got through the opening just as the lead lion's massive head slammed against it. The lion tried to shove its way through, but its head was simply too big.

At that moment three rapid sounds of *phwtt* were heard, and the lions staggered. Chuck turned his head and saw Paul, cradling the trank rifle, which was covered with dust. When a circus goes so long without the slightest hint of trouble, even routine safety measures become forgotten.

The lions began to stagger around, and one of them promptly slumped over.

"Jesus God, look at those bars," Gwynn was saying.

"Shut up about the bars! Get a doctor! Get a goddamn ambulance!" Dakota was shouting, for the mauled Harry was breathing irregularly, and his body was covered with huge, ugly cuts. His left forearm looked somewhat chewed.

The grandstands were still filled, and the shouting and talking in the tent was now almost deafening. No one had left. After all, if someone were eaten by a lion, that would certainly be something no one would want to miss. Tell the grandkids. Make a day of it.

Dakota tilted back Chuck's head, trying to staunch the bleeding, while the carnival doctor quickly applied first aid to Harry. Already, faintly, in the distance, the *shreee* of the ambulance could be heard. "God, Chuck, that was the bravest thing I've ever seen anyone do." She was cradling his head in her lap and, despite himself, he enjoyed the warmth of her.

Paul was staring at one of the slumped over lions. "That lion has two darts in it," he said.

Gwynn looked up from the bars. "You shot him twice. So?"

"No, I shot him once. Each of them once. Where'd the second one come from."

Slowly Chuck turned toward Rommel. The large dog's fur was matted with blood.

"You all right?"

I'll live. The extra dart . . . you think . . . ?

"Yeah," Chuck said. "Somebody shot the lions from the stands. Shot them with some sort of stimulants. Drove them berserk."

Dakota naturally assumed he'd been talking to her. Her face blanched. "Chuck, that's . . . that's crazy! Who would do that?"

He knew. It was someone who was willing to jeopardize, even sacrifice, the life of an innocent lion tamer, just to see if Chuck was really at the carnival. Because, obviously, they had known that Chuck wouldn't just stand by and let someone be killed if he could help it.

And although he knew that the opening of the locked door wouldn't be noticed by his friends, and the high leap and even the bar bending would easily be chalked off to adrenalin, there were definitely others who would recognize those feats for what they were.

Chuck stared with quiet certainty at Rommel. "Whoever it was . . . they're gone now."

"You think so?" said Dakota uncertainly.

"Yeah, I do."

You're right, came from Rommel. *But they'll be back.*

And Chuck nodded slowly. Rommel was absolutely right. Now that they knew that he was here . . . they would be back.

In force.

September 8, 2020

2

SUN STREAMED THROUGH the window of Chuck Simon's bedroom, which was an unusual enough event in itself. What was even more unusual was that Chuck was in bed to be there when the sunlight hit him.

Chuck moaned and rolled over, instinctively turning his head away from the bothersome light so that he could get some more sleep. He scratched himself, snorted slightly, and then, half-asleep, realization struck him.

He sat up very quickly, blinking furiously. Sunlight? *Sunlight?* What time was it?

He glanced at the alarm clock on the night stand and gasped, "Oh my God." In friendly, glowing letters it informed him that it was 7:22 A.M. What it didn't bother to tell him was that school started in just over half an hour.

But he had set the alarm! His fist slammed down on the clock and, promptly, sickly sweet country music poured out of it.

There was no better time to discover that you needed a new alarm clock than on your first day back to work.

And he was doubly annoyed because he always liked to get in a run first thing in the morning. Usually his internal clock was more than enough to get him up at five-thirty, and by six o'clock he was running his five miles, a familiar sight to other residents of LeQuier, Ohio. He would wave to the kids on their paper routes or to the men on the various service trucks making their early morning deliveries. Nice, comfortable, and secure. A pleasant way to avoid the knowledge that so many parts of the country had gone down the chute.

Now, though, there was certainly no time for that. Chuck kicked away the sheets, leaped out of bed, and dashed naked to the bathroom. He grabbed the toothbrush, toothpaste, and a paper cup, rushed into the glass-enclosed shower and let the water run over him while he brushed his teeth. The toothpaste he spat out mixed with the water that swirled sludgily down the drain.

He stepped out of the shower and noticed a thin, dark film building up on the glass door. As he toweled himself down he made a mental reminder to swing by the hardware store and pick up a new purifying tablet for the shower head. It was annoying as hell—one tablet was supposed to last for three months, and Chuck was sure that it had barely been two since he'd installed the last one. Which either meant that the water was getting worse or the tablets were getting less effective.

After finishing in the bathroom, he ran out onto the hardwood floor that led from the bathroom to the closer of two bedrooms in the small frame house. He skidded slightly, his feet still wet. But he righted himself, snagging the door frame, and then dashed into the bedroom.

Minutes later he was wearing his customary work clothes—a gray t-shirt with *LeQuier High School* stenciled in a semicircle over his heart, and neatly pressed gray running pants. He finished lacing up his sneakers and glanced out the window.

Naturally the sunlight had been fleeting. The customary

gray overcast (which had become so prevalent that it was the official school color) now lined the skies once more.

In the background he had the radio on, which informed him that the air was breathable today. That was a nice change of pace, and certainly a good way to start off school. During the year, whenever it was stated that the air was not quality air, over half his classes started claiming that they couldn't exercise because they couldn't breathe. Of course the warnings applied mainly to the elderly and very small children, not lazy jocks. But it gave them something to grouse about.

How nice they wouldn't have it for the first day.

Chuck finished tying his sneakers, and then he yanked on his warm-up jacket and ran out the door, slamming it shut behind him.

He ran to the driveway and stopped.

His car was gone.

A flash of panic ran through him and then he remembered. It was in the shop. The anti-pollution devices had seized up, and Chuck had had a narrow escape when he'd realized just in time that carbon monoxide had been backing up into the car through the air conditioner. He had intended, this day, to take the bus.

Just spiffy. Still, if he didn't have to wait for one, he could still just barely make it to school.

He glanced at his watch. He'd managed to get up, washed, dressed, and out in eight minutes flat. Certainly he could make two blocks fast enough to catch the bus that came in around seven-thirty. It was always a couple of minutes late anyway.

Naturally, this day it was punctual.

Chuck rounded the corner just in time to see the bus at the stop and a woman's leg disappearing through the doors.

Within a moment the doors would close and the bus would pull out.

Chuck shouted, but his voice was lost in the roar of the engine as the bus prepared to lurch forward.

Please don't close, Chuck thought desperately, his feet pounding on the pavement.

He ran desperately toward the bus, praying that the doors wouldn't shut and the bus would remain where it was.

And miraculously, the bus sat there waiting for him. It started forward, went a couple of feet, and rolled to a halt, the doors still open.

Chuck ran up and leaped in through the doors, snagging the railing. He grinned lopsidedly and said, "Made it!" to no one in particular.

The driver, for his part, didn't seem to care. He was struggling with the lever and he snapped, "You could've walked it. The door's stuck. I can't close it. I'll have to put the bus out of ser—"

And at that moment the lever suddenly swung to the right and the doors promptly closed.

The driver, a large, beefy man who didn't like being jerked around by a bus, experimentally opened and closed the door a couple of times. No problem.

"You're a lucky bastard," grunted the driver.

"I know," sighed Chuck in relief as he inserted his card into the slotbox next to the driver. A small red light shifted to green, indicating the card had been scanned and approved. The driver put the bus into gear and it started forward.

Chuck made his way to the back of the bus, since most of the other seats were occupied by sullen-looking individuals for whom the first day of school meant little else than pleasant (or unpleasant, depending upon how you did in those days) memories of school years and traumas long past. He plopped into a rear seat and looked out the back window.

A huge billow of black, noxious smoke was rising up from behind them. Chuck frowned and looked down as blackness belched from the tailpipe.

"Excuse me!" Chuck called out. Heads turned to look at him. "Excuse me, driver!"

"What?" the driver said. It was clear that he was not in the greatest of moods.

"You're letting out a lot of black smoke. It has to be far more than the limit."

"Yeah? So?"

"So you should get it fixed."

"I did get it fixed," laughed the driver from the front.

Immediately Chuck knew what had happened. Many people complained about the various anti-pollution devices on buses and cars these days. Not only were malfunctions, such as Chuck's, potentially lethal, but supposedly they also interfered with the engine. For example, cars stalled out a great deal because of the devices. They really needed work and had been rushed into production too soon, but as the anti-pollution furor had risen, the government had had to do something. It was, of course, too little, too late.

What the driver had doubtlessly done was have the anti-pollution devices removed, rationalizing it for a whole array of reasons. Bottom line was, it was against the law.

"I'm sorry, sir," said Chuck, "but unless you promise you'll have this attended to, I'll have to have you reported."

"Oh, really." Suddenly the driver was sounding very unpleasant.

"Yes, sir," said Chuck.

The bus angled toward the curb and Chuck noted that there was no bus stop there.

The driver turned in his seat and said, "Get out."

There were moans from people on the bus. They didn't want a confrontation. They wanted to get to work.

"I beg your pardon?" said Chuck.

"Out," said the driver. He had gotten up from his seat, and Chuck noted that the driver was considerably larger and definitely heavier than he was.

"Is there a problem?"

"You bet there's a problem. No Extremists on my bus."

"I assure you sir," said Chuck calmly, "I am not an Extremist."

The driver walked toward Chuck and stopped a foot or so away. The people in the bus were expressing various forms of dissatisfaction now, some siding with the driver, others telling the driver to just leave the guy alone, and all of them wishing that either Chuck or the driver would just *do* something already to bring the nonsense to an end.

It became quickly evident, however, that neither of them was about to back down.

"I think you *are* an Extremist," snarled the driver. "One of those guys who goes around blowing up factories and shit."

"I have better things to do with my time—" Chuck noted the nameplate that was pinned to the driver's shirt, just above the large stain from the coffee that the driver had spilled on himself early that morning—"Mr. Mahoney. I'm just someone who, if he sees something that he knows is wrong, can't turn a blind eye to it."

"Oh, really," said Mahoney.

And from behind Mahoney now came a voice that Chuck recognized as belonging to Bob Higgins. His son, Horace—commonly known as "Hog"—was one of the pre-

miere centers in the football lineup of the high school.
"Come on, driver, leave the guy alone," said Higgins.
"He's harmless. He's the school coach. How you doing,
Coach? We going all the way this year?"

Chuck raised a fist in solid, kick-ass affirmation.

"I don't care who he is, he's a troublemaker."

"For pity's sake, driver, the guy's a pacificst. He's a
Quaker," said Higgins.

Chuck raised an eyebrow at that. Although he'd never
gone out of his way to conceal his background, he'd never
exactly hyped it, either. Surprising to discover what people are aware of.

Mahoney looked at Chuck askance. "I thought you guys
lived in Pennsylvania. And wore funny clothes and shit."

Chuck was suddenly getting very tired of this. Tired of
all eyes on the bus directed at him. Tired of this driver
spewing his coffee-rich breath at him. Tired of the fact
that he'd managed to catch the damned bus and he was
going to be late anyway, thanks to this bullying, all because he'd felt constrained to bear witness to the polluting
by the bus.

Good lord, everything was so polluted as it was anyway.
Sure they were trying to clamp down on auto emissions,
but in the meantime, factories manufacturing weapons and
God knows what other toxic wastes were springing up
thanks to the wars. And since they were government-
sponsored, controls were loose to non-existent. Not to
mention the perpetual haze from the nuclear plant that had
blown up in Seattle. They had neutralized the radiation,
sure, but the ash still hung there, high in the atmosphere.
An atmosphere already ozone depleted and—

God, in view of all that, what the devil did one stupid
bus have to do with anything? Why was he bothering anyway?

He sighed inwardly. Because he had seen it and should do something about it. No other reason.

He tossed his mind back to what the driver had just said, about Pennsylvania and ''shit.''

''That's the Amish,'' he said tiredly. ''But we do share their feeling that aggression is not the way to do things.''

''Well good,'' snapped Mahoney, fed up. ''So get your non-aggressive ass off my bus, now.''

He grabbed Chuck's left upper arm with his right hand.

That was his first mistake.

His second mistake was not fully realizing the differences between Amish and Quakers.

Chuck's reaction was automatic. He brought his other hand up, pressed Mahoney's hand against his own arm to keep the driver's hand in place. Then he swung his left arm up so that he now had leverage.

The driver didn't realize yet he was in serious trouble. That was because less than a second had passed, and Chuck hadn't even risen from his seat. But now Chuck leaned forward slightly, and to Mahoney's confused shock, his own arm bent back. He twisted around in place, as if weightless, and suddenly the floor was coming up at him. He slammed face first into it, the thud reverberating up and down the aisle. People gasped and cried out, and two, including Higgins, applauded.

The human arm was not meant to bend that way, and muscle twisted against bone. Not only was the driver immobilized by the pain that ripped through his socket, but Chuck was calmly holding Mahoney's right wrist joint in an unbreakable grip that kept Mahoney pinned, agonized and helpless. Mahoney's nose rubbed in the dirt and crud that collected on the floor, and he had a good view of an assortment of hardened gum wads stuck under the nearest seat.

"I really don't want to hurt you," said Chuck.

Mahoney tried to twist away and only succeeded in injuring himself more as the arm continued to try and bend in a direction nature had not intended. He let out a shriek. "Help me, you motherfucking bastards!" he shouted.

Unsurprisingly, no one felt constrained to leap to his aid.

"If I let you go, you will go back to driving, and you will have the pollution device attended to," said Chuck calmly.

"You can kiss my *aahhhhhhh*—!" he howled as Chuck applied the slightest of pressure.

"I really don't like doing this," said Chuck, and he sounded sincere.

"Then stop it! *Stop it!*"

"As soon as you—"

"All right!" bellowed Mahoney. "I'll do it! You can check with my supervisor! I swear to God, I'll do it!"

"Good."

Chuck released him and slid back into his seat, his hands folded neatly in his lap. Mahoney lay there a moment, then tried to get up, using his arm for support. This was less than a success and he hit the floor again. The next time he reared back on his hind quarters, rubbing the shoulder to restart circulation.

He cast a sullen glance at Chuck, then got up and went to the front of the bus. The air brakes hissed and, without a word, he swung the bus back out onto the road.

Chuck sat serenly in his seat, endeavoring to take no notice of the fact that passengers seemed to be trying to give him a wider berth. He smiled inwardly at that. Obviously they were concerned that he might go berserk at any time and leap into them, tearing them apart with a combination of vicious hand chops to the throat and groin.

All accompanied, of course, by high-pitched screams à la an old Bruce Lee film.

Honestly.

Higgins, however, had stitched together his nerve and moved over to a seat right next to Chuck's. Chuck nodded his head in acknowledgement.

In a low whisper, Higgins said, "What was that you did to him?"

Chuck really did not see much purpose in dwelling on it. An act of violence, even one that was self-defense, was not something to be reveled in, or discussed *ad infinitum*. That was not the way toward maintaining balance of the soul and spirit.

Still, it was quite evident that Higgins was not going to dematerialize. Besides, he *had* tried to intercede on Chuck's behalf. That certainly entailed as much courtesy as Chuck could provide.

"Tomiki aikido," said Chuck.

Higgins frowned. "Who's she?"

Chuck tried to suppress a smile and only partly succeeded. "It's a form of martial art."

"You mean like karate?"

"Not ex—"

"You kick and punch people and stuff?"

"It's—"

He tried to figure out a way to explain it in terms Higgins would understand. "It's a fighting style that emphasizes grace of movement, form, and harmony," he said. "There are no offensive moves. It's used only for defense."

"You're kidding. No punching?"

"No."

"Then what good is it?"

Chuck tossed a glance in the direction of the floor, reminding Higgins of what had happened only moments before. "Yeah, good point," conceded Higgins. "Still—I like karate. Not that I know it, although, y'know, you pick up some moves from the TV and such. Sometimes there's no substitute for a punch in the face."

"Sure there is."

"Yeah? What?"

Chuck smiled. "A kiss to the face."

"Yeah, well," snorted Higgins, "I didn't see you kissing that bus driver."

"He's not my type," said Chuck, laughing.

"No running in the hallway!"

Chuck skidded to a halt, his sneakers making rubber screeching noises. The echoes of the final bell were just fading. The hallway of the high school had emptied out, the last of the homeroom doors closing with a guillotine finality that indicated the first day of school had begun.

The voice registered on him just before he turned. "I'm sorry," he said in an alarmed falsetto, "I don't have a hall pass. Don't expel me, please!"

Linda Hollaway slowly strolled toward him, her denim skirt swishing attractively around her knees, her roman sandals laced up to mid-calf. She had an attendance book held against her white sweater, the sleeves pushed up and scrunched around her elbows. Her blonde hair was cut much shorter than Chuck remembered. Her skin was also several shades browner.

"Oh, we're going to do worse than expel you," she said sternly, a smile betraying the serious tone of her voice. "We're going to . . . give you a homeroom!"

"No!" moaned Chuck.

"And make you teach gym!"

"Oh, God," Chuck staggered, bumping against the lockers. "Not gym! Those that can, do. Those that can't, teach. And those that can't teach, teach gym."

She grinned now, turning the full force of that dazzling smile on him. "How you doing, Chuck?"

"Not as good as you, Linda."

"As *well* as you."

He rolled his eyes. Lord save him from English teachers. "I haven't checked in at the office yet."

"Well you don't have time," and she linked an arm around his elbow and started briskly down the hallway. She was a head shorter than the burly coach, but she seemed to be dragging him as if he were weightless. "Come on. Your homeroom assignment's this way. I'm in A-30. You're in A-20, Feiser's old room. He went to Chicago, you know."

"That hell hole?" Chuck said in disbelief.

"He said he wanted a challenge."

"I could do without challenges like that," he replied. "How do you know where my homeroom is?"

"I checked." At his look, she said, "I knew you would be late. You're always late for the first day. Thought I'd do you a favor."

"Well, thanks. You do look great, by the way."

"Three months," she said, "on the coast of Greece. Beautiful little house that I shared with a girlfriend. Did nothing but relax, swim, luxuriate on the beach."

"That sure explains the tan."

"All over," she purred. "Care to check?"

"Some other time."

"Consider it a standing invitation."

"Here's your homeroom," he said quickly.

She hadn't noticed, and was slightly dismayed that he

had been paying more attention to room numbers than to her.

As if anticipating her next comment, Chuck said, "We can talk about it later," and hurried quickly down the hallway. She shrugged, opened the door, and went inside, the student chatter promptly dying down upon her entrance.

Chuck, despite the rules, ran the rest of the way. He paused at the door, his hand on the knob, and listened to voices. He recognized a lot of them. God, they'd stuck all the jocks in his homeroom. What kind of sadist had come up with that?

He steeled himself and opened the door.

Sure enough, there they were, about a dozen strong, clustered toward the back of the class. They were laughing, chortling, punching each other on the shoulders—a sea of gray varsity jackets. Sure enough, there was Hog Higgins himself, in the thick of it. Then they all looked up to see Chuck.

Like a bull moose in heat, Hog bellowed *"COOOOAAACH!"* and immediately the others started shouting it too, pounding on the desk tops rhythmically as they chanted, faster and faster, "Coach coach coach coach coachcoachcoachcoach . . ."

Chuck raised his hands, as if surrendering to the accolades, and they all cheered. "Save it!" Chuck called. "Save it for the pep rallies, okay?"

"This is the first one!" declared Hog. Next to him, Marty Turret, a.k.a. Turbine, nodded in agreement. Turbine was usually nodding in agreement with Hog. Generally the only time he wasn't was when he was asleep and maybe, for all Chuck knew, then also.

Chuck abruptly realized he didn't have an attendance

book, thanks to his bypassing the office. "Anyone have paper and pen they can lend me?"

There were twenty-five students in the room. They all looked blank.

"Oh, come on, people," sighed Chuck. "It's the first day of school. How can you come with nothing to write with?"

"You did," pointed out Hog. It drew a chuckle.

Taking pity on Chuck, Rona Slater withdrew the requested writing implements from her bag and handed them up to him.

"All right, people," he said. "First thing is, I think we should all get reacquainted. I want you all to turn around and shake hands with the person behind you."

Chuck was pleased to see that some old gags still worked as all the students turned and extended their right hands only to find themselves staring at the backs of the people behind them who were doing the same thing. The jocks in the back were actually thick enough to turn and look toward the wall.

A kind of free-floating, dry "Oh ha ha ha" floated through the room, and Chuck grinned at that. "Now then," he said, and sat down. "One at a time, call out your name. I'll write 'em down, and compare them with the master list later. Starting with you," and he pointed at one girl, and gestured that it should follow down to the end of her row and around.

As the name announcing swept around the room, Rory Gunderman, who was seated next to Hog Higgins, quietly wadded up a spitball. Rory wasn't much for football, but he was the best pitcher on the baseball team. Hog grinned lopsidedly when he saw what Rory was up to. Sure Hog liked the coach just fine, but that didn't mean he wasn't above having some fun with him.

Rory drew back and let fly.

Just as he did, Chuck looked up, as if warned.

The fastball turned into a curve, sailing just wide of Chuck's face and splatting into the chalkboard.

Chuck glanced at the dripping wad with mild interest. "Was that supposed to be your high heat, Rory?" he asked.

"Uh . . ." Rory shrugged, embarrassed. "Yeah."

"Seems you're having trouble telling your ace from your deuce," Chuck observed. "Control problems should be nipped in the bud. Know what's good for that?"

Rory shook his head, but had a sinking feeling he knew. As it turned out, he was right.

"Building up the arm muscles," Chuck said, "as with push-ups. Like the extra hundred you'll give me during gym." He smiled. "Any problem with that?"

"No, Coach," said Rory, the picture of misery. Next to him, Hog chuckled.

"Don't worry, Rory," said Chuck. "It won't be so bad. Hog will be keeping you company. Right, Hog?"

"Why me?!" cried out Hog in indignation.

"Because you thought it was funny. And because you saw Rory making the spitball and just sat by and let it happen."

"How do you know?" demanded Hog.

With an utter deadpan, Chuck said, "I know everything."

Hog slumped back in his chair in irritation and, inwardly, Chuck smiled.

The last of the students called out his name and Chuck, whose hand was starting to cramp up, finished writing it. He studied the list momentarily.

"I got every one of you hot-shot athletes except for Zack Jordan? Who got Zack?"

And now there was a sort of disconcerted uncomfortableness in the room, and immediately Chuck's antenna went up. "Is Zack supposed to be here?" he said slowly. "There's no point in covering for him, guys. If Zack should be here, I'll find out about it sooner or later. Hog? You want to fill me in?"

Hog shrugged with those massive shoulders of his. "Nothing to fill in, Coach," he said. "No one's seen Zack around much lately. That's all."

"Where is he?"

"I don't know," said Hog with impatience, and Chuck sensed that Hog was telling the truth. More than that—he had the distinct feeling that Hog was nervous, even frightened for Zack.

This was something that Chuck was going to have to look into.

3

CHIEF OF POLICE Ed Slezak glanced up from his cluttered desk. Slezak was heavyset, with a perpetual film of perspiration on his high forehead. He peered through his glasses at the individual who was standing in front of him.

The man was wearing a long tweed coat, which made sense since it was pretty brisk outside. But his hat was pulled down low, and his sunglasses were tinted cobalt blue. These days, few people wore sunglasses, what with the sun being an almost forgotten astronomical phenomenon.

"Excuse me," said Slezak, not bothering to hide his annoyance. "But this is my office. You can't just come wandering in here. Who let you in?"

When the man spoke his voice was soft, a carefully cultivated tone that sounded as if it was just above a whisper. But there was definitely a feeling of restrained—what? Power? Anger? "I let myself in," he said.

"Then," said Slezak, rising and hitching up his belt, "you can damn well just let yourself right back out again."

The man extended a small, black billfold and flipped it open. Slezak glanced without too much interest at the identification that was inside, but he was stunned when he looked at it more closely. For a moment he thought that perhaps the ID was fake. But something told him—perhaps it was the combination of the ID and the man himself—warned him, that it was all too genuine.

He looked back at the man, and he fought down the surge of fear. He tried not to let his voice quaver as he said. "Wh—what can I do for you, Mr. . . ." He glanced at the ID once more. "Mr. Quint."

"Chuck Simon," said the man softly, flipping the bill-fold closed and returning it smoothly to his jacket pocket.

"You mean Coach?"

"Yes. Coach."

"Nice young man," said Slezak.

"You think so?"

"Well, that is," amended Slezak quickly, "I can't say as I know him all that well. I mean, it's not like I'd go to bat for him. I mean, it's not like, if you guys say he's up to something, I could tell you for sure that he's not. Hey, for all I know, he's up to something. Is he?"

As if Slezak had not even spoken, Quint said, "I want you to do something for me."

"Anything. If I can cooperate in any way—"

"If Chuck Simon comes by, reports problems of any sort—ignore him."

"Ignore him?" Slezak didn't understand.

"Be polite, but brush him off."

Slezak started to ask why, but caught himself. If there was one thing you didn't ask people like Quint, it was why they wanted things done.

Slezak had heard rumors of what happened to people who'd questioned people like Quint. People who had dis-appeared one day, swallowed up by the government, or what passed for the government these days.

"We would very much appreciate your cooperation," said Quint.

"You—you would?"

"Substantially," said Quint. "For example, when you check your credit balance on your card next, you will discover an additional five thousand extension."

Slezak blinked and sank down into his seat. It had been eating at him, that he was so near his limit. His salary, which was directly applied each week to his balance—as it was with everyone—was barely making a dent in the outstanding amount he owed. Food shopping had seemed almost impossible the end of this week, and he hadn't figured out a way to tell his wife yet.

But a five thousand extension? That would take care of him for months. For—

He stopped. Was this a bribe? Was it unsavory somehow?

No. It couldn't be. Because it came from someone like Quint, and the people he represented, hell, they never broke the laws. They made the laws. They were the laws.

"How did you know?" said Slezak. "How did you know how badly off I was?"

"It's my job to know," replied Quint. "It's what I do. And what you can do is what I tell you. Do we understand each other?"

"Yes, sir," said Slezak, head bobbing up and down like one of those little toys with the head on a spring.

"Good." Quint did not smile. He never did. "I'm glad we were able to come to an understanding."

4

CAREFULLY BALANCING HIS tray, Chuck sidled into the teachers' cafeteria lounge and looked for an open table.

When he'd been a kid, Chuck had wondered about the mysteries that lay behind the doors of various teachers' lounges. As opposed to the spartan bleakness of other aspects of student life, he had imagined that the teachers' lounges had everything short of a Jacuzzi, and maybe even that. He envisioned plush couches, chairs, recreational facilities—everything that one could ask for.

What there was, of course, was not much of anything. The one couch had had the same spring sticking out of the same cushion for at least three years, and the tables and chairs were of pretty much the same (lack of) quality one would find in the student cafeteria.

Linda Hollaway was across the room and was waving to Chuck that he should join her. Chuck bobbed his head and threaded his way across as other teachers smiled acknowledgment or greeted him verbally.

He dropped his tray down opposite Linda and she glanced at it appraisingly. "You actually got the salisbury steak," she said. "God, the only thing worse than that is the chuckwagon."

"I like the chuckwagon," he protested.

"Nobody knows what it is."

"Well, that's what I like about it," he retorted.

As he started to eat, Linda said, "So . . . what did you do with your summer?"

He glanced up at her and actually looked embarrassed. "You'll laugh," he said.

"No, I won't."

"You will."

"Cross my heart."

He paused. "I went to school at the University. I'm working toward my Masters so I can get to be assistant principal."

She stared at him, her lips forcibly pressed together to stifle it. He watched her for a long moment and then sighed, "Oh, go ahead."

She laughed delightedly.

"Feel better?"

"Hold it," she said, putting up a hand and trying not to choke. "Give me a minute."

Chuck waited patiently until she'd recovered herself. "You?" she finally managed to get out. "Assistant principal?"

"You don't think I can do it?"

"I don't know why you'd *want* to do it. It's an awful job. Dealing with cranky parents, cranky kids, and all the garbage that Olivetti wants to pass on, which is most of it. Besides, and don't take this wrong, but I've never, in any school I've been at, seen a gym teacher promoted to A. P."

At that moment there was a deep, throat-clearing cough behind them. Linda turned and looked up and saw the ominous Olivetti looming over them.

Olivetti, the principal, was a few inches over six feet

tall. His brown hair was a bristly crew cut, and his pock-marked face showed signs of a lost battle with acne in his youth.

What Olivetti did best, in his role as principal, was loom. He did it now, and Linda hoped to hell that he hadn't heard the comment about how he liked to pass on most of his work.

"You're looking tanned, Linda," he said.

"She's tanned all over," said Chuck helpfully. "She offered to show me. Maybe she'd like to show you."

Linda fired a deadly glance at Chuck, who smiled ingenuously.

"Some other time, perhaps," said Olivetti. He had not come down there to eat lunch—he never ate lunch with the teachers, but always secluded in his office. No one knew what he ate. Nails, probably. "Coach . . ."

"Yes, sir."

"You're history."

Alarmed, Linda looked from Olivetti to Chuck, but Chuck was grinning and he clapped his hands together. "Excellent!"

Linda was completely confused. "What?"

"I got Brown's history class," Chuck said.

Now Linda understood. Wendy Brown was eight months pregnant, and would be going on maternity leave shortly. She taught U.S. history, and they'd be needing a substitute.

But . . . Chuck?

"I'm going out on a bit of a limb for you, Coach," Olivetti told him. "If grade point averages drop off in history, parents are going to be after my hide because I put the gym coach in charge of the class."

"I'll be prepared, sir," said Chuck earnestly. "And I want to thank you for the opportunity."

"Two weeks," Olivetti told him, not particularly interested in Chuck's profuse thanks. "Wendy will be departing in two weeks, barring premature labor. Be sure to get together with her, perhaps observe her class for several days. It's a ten-thirty class, so I presume it will not interfere with one of your phys. ed. classes?"

Chuck shook his head, but he knew that Olivetti must have already been aware of it. Very little went on in the school that Olivetti didn't know about. Which reminded Chuck . . .

"Sir," he said, "what's going on with Zack Jordan?"

Olivetti frowned at that. "His behavior has been very erratic," he said. "It started about a week or so ago, a very recent development. His mother's on the school board, you know. She said he just seems to stare off into space. That he's become short tempered, extra-aggressive, and sometimes just plain antisocial."

Linda was shrugging. "Sounds like a typical teenager to me."

But Chuck wasn't looking at it that way. Zack had been a pretty reliable, solid kid. Most of the kids in LeQuier were, really, and Zack was no different. Could there be problems at home? Chuck had also met the mother a couple of times in her professional capacity, but not Chuck's father. Still, LeQuier was small—if there were trouble at Zack's house, it would be common knowledge.

"I think," said Chuck, "that maybe I'll try and track him down. Have a chat with him."

"He's always respected you, Coach," said Olivetti dourly. "Perhaps he'll listen. Either way, it's good to see you endeavoring to take responsibility. That's a valued commodity for an assistant principal." He nodded once more and walked off.

Linda watched Olivetti's retreating form and turned in

wonderment to Chuck. "My God . . . he actually likes you."

"Doesn't everybody?" smiled Chuck.

"Yeah, but . . . Olivetti? The Dragon Man?" She shook her head. "He knows about this University thing you've got going?"

He nodded. "High school's picking up part of the tuition, since it's training for a job here at the school."

"Not bad. Where you getting the rest of the money?"

"Some I saved up. And the rest wherever I can. For example," and he shook his head at the memory, "I participated in some psych experiments."

"Like what? Rorschach blots and stuff?"

"More like these things where they are looking at cards on the other side of a partition, and you're supposed to guess what's on the card? Like, there's a symbol of a star, and three wavy lines—"

"Oh, right! Right, I've heard about things like that," she said. "It's ESP tests. You're supposed to try and figure out the card by picking up thought projections. So how'd you do?"

"I don't know," shrugged Chuck. "I guess I did all right. Most people participated for a day or so, but they kept me coming back for a week. They seemed very interested. Doesn't surprise me, I guess. I've always been kind of lucky with that sort of thing. You know me—Mr. Mind Reader."

"Has it ever occurred to you that maybe you *are* psychic?" she said teasingly. "You never know."

He laughed at that. "People are so imaginative."

"Hey, you brought it up."

"Yeah, but I was kidding around. People always want to ascribe routine feelings and emotions to something other than what it is. A low-flying plane becomes a UFO. Re-

membering a situation similar to one you're in becomes
déjà vu. Imagine someone's in trouble and the one time
out of a million you're right, you think you're precogni-
tive. It's all nonsense. Things happen naturally, and they
happen when they happen, and no one can see the future,
and that's all there is.''

"Pity. I'd love to see the future.''

"Really,'' he grinned. "What would you want to see in
it?''

"I'd want to see if we're going to go out together.''

He leaned back and sighed. "Linda—I'm not ready yet.
I'm sorry, but—''

She shook her head in exasperation. "Chucky—I think
it's about time you faced facts. Your wife isn't coming
back. Anna left you three years ago and divorced you six
months later. Now I've been politely interested ever since,
and I've been getting just as polite brush-offs from you.
If it's because you're just not interested in me, please tell
me so that I can stop embarrassing myself. If it's that
you're still hoping that Anna will realize the error of her
ways, then for pity's sake, grow up and stop embarrassing
yourself.''

She sat back in her chair, and then became aware of a
lot of eyes upon her. She slowly looked behind her and
realized that she'd been a tad louder than she'd intended.
Everyone in the lounge was looking at her, and thank
heaven Olivetti had left already. "Somebody got something to say?'' she asked challengingly, and there were
quick shakings of heads, combined with quite a few
smirks.

Chuck hadn't moved, but there was a rueful smile on
his face. "You're right, of course,'' he admitted. "Look
. . . it's—''

"No, forget it,'' she put up a hand. "It's none of my

business. I shouldn't have said anything. I was out of line. Okay? Forget I opened my big mouth.''

She got up, taking her tray with her, and left the faculty lounge. Chuck stayed where he was, staring sadly into open air.

Was it true? God, *was* he still thinking about Anna? How can you be haunted by the ghost of someone who was still alive? Who had stepped all over your feelings? Who had fled the town you had chosen to live in because life just wasn't exciting enough there for her?

He hadn't heard from her in months and wondered what she was up to. Had she found something exciting enough for her? Considering what was going on in the big cities, with all the terrorism and insanity, he had not been quite able to figure out why anyone would want to leave the calm and security of a small town like theirs.

Perhaps she didn't want calm and security. So what was he supposed to provide her then? Chaos?

Not possible. Chuck had worked too long and hard— continued to work, in fact—on maintaining a balance of personality and nature. He was calm and at peace. He wanted, needed, harmony. Not discord.

If discord was what Anna had wanted, then it was best that they had split.

So why was there a hole in his chest?

It was a week later when Chuck spotted Zack outside the school.

He had seen the young man briefly, flitting through the hallway, sticking his head through an open doorway and then disappearing. He hadn't had the opportunity to catch up with him, and besides, what was he supposed to do? Throw a lasso over him and hogtie him?

This time, however, Chuck had been at the school quite

late. He had been preparing lesson plans for his upcoming first days as a history teacher, and found he was most comfortable in his small office. The distinctive aroma that radiated from the boy's locker room did not distract him at all, so used to it was he by this time. He had piled his desk high with books and was reviewing key points to be discussed.

He flipped through a section on the Constitution and stopped at the Bill of Rights. He shook his head sadly. He knew that there had been a time when they were important, back before they had been suspended. Oddly enough, there had been tremendous protest about it at the time, but eventually the protests had died down as months turned into years and the temporary injunction slowly set into hardened stone.

What had been given up, he wondered? Not much, really, when he thought about it. Oh, people older than he were always clucking about it, grumbling about free speech and things like that. But when the injunction had been made by the president, Chuck was too young to fully understand what was happening. So as he grew up, he didn't feel as if he'd been missing anything.

Matters weren't so bad, really. Sure, things were strict. But with all the Extremists running around, the terrorists—both third world and environmental—and such, stricter regulation was necessary. The population simply had to be kept under firmer control, and certainly the minority had made it necessary for the majority, but that's just the way life was.

It was that need for security that had led to the Cards. Everyone was issued a Card at birth. The initial idea was that it was like a birth certificate, except you carried it with you at all times. Your Card was imprinted with your retina pattern. Not only did it enable you to prove your identity and citizenship, but it allowed the government to keep total and complete track of the comings and goings of all citizens. This, of course, led to increased safety and security.

For example, you could not get on an airplane without presenting your Card. While you were checked to make certain you were indeed the authorized carrier of the Card, a cross-check was also done almost instantaneously with the government computers. If the computers informed airline personnel that you were a security risk—history of terrorism, for example, or fleeing from some sort of charge—then you were taken away and—

And what? Chuck wondered. He'd always been a bit unclear on that. People the government did not approve of occasionally just disappeared. You never knew quite where or why. But Chuck was certain this was not wrong, because the government would only take you away if you had done something that warranted it.

Certainly crime was down. The jails were no longer overcrowded—there seemed to be far fewer prisoners, and the ones that were there always seemed to be the ones who committed the more petty crimes. The serious offenders, the career criminals that Chuck heard once constituted the majority of prisoners—they had dropped off to insignificant numbers.

Bill of Rights. Chuck made a derisive noise. Certainly the Elders in the Society of Friends church that Chuck regularly attended would sometimes wax nostalgic for the Bill of Rights. Then again, they also became wistful sometimes for some music group called the Beatles that apparently British Prime Minister McCartney had once belonged to. So who could tell what was important and what wasn't?

Well, he was going to have to, he realized. As history

teacher, it was his job to sort fact from fallacy, truth from half-truth. He did not want to let the kids down.

He sorted through other books, including out-of-date texts on currency. Now there had been another superb idea. Once the ID nature of the Cards had worked out so well, hard money had fallen into such disuse that it was practically obsolete. Everyone had accounts tied in to their cards, and salaries were paid directly into those accounts. Every purchase was deducted from the accounts, as were charges for such services as phone, electricity, and ash removal.

Everything was so much simpler these days.

He looked up from his work, wondering why it was beginning to get dark in his office, and realized that it was well after six. He packed up a few books, stuffed them into his carry bag, and hurried out the back of the school.

He made his way through the deserted parking lot, relieved that within the next day or so his car would be repaired and he could give up this bus business. He started to turn left and then caught something from the corner of his eye to the right.

He recognized the posture immediately. It was Zack Jordan. He was talking to someone who was cloaked in the darkness of the evening. There was something about him. . . . Chuck couldn't put his finger on it, but it made him extremely uncomfortable.

Chuck started toward the two of them, half anticipating that one or the other might bolt upon seeing him.

Neither did, though, and moments later Chuck had neared them. He stopped roughly two arm lengths away from the closest of them, which happened to be the man in darkness.

Chuck was more than uncomfortable now. There was a deep feeling of dislike, even free-floating dread.

The three of them stood there silently for a long moment and then Chuck turned his attention toward Zack.

Zack looked out of it. He was wavering slightly in place, his eyes unfocussed. He had always been a robust youth, but now an aura of defeat hung over him like a shroud. His red hair was disheveled, his jersey tucked half in, half out.

"Zack," he said slowly. "Haven't seen you around much."

Zack stared at him, a quizzical expression on his face, and Chuck realized with growing alarm that Zack didn't even recognize him. Part of him wanted to grab Zack, shake him, scream "What's the matter with you!?" right in his face.

But he did not. Instead he reached into himself, reached for the calm center, for balance. "Zack, you want to introduce me to your friend?"

With Chuck's eyes adjusting to the darkness, he could make more of Zack's companion out now. He was wearing a short windbreaker and a cap pulled low over his eyes. All his clothes were black, as if he were part of the night. His face was grizzled, his eyes seemed to swim in a pool of darkness. "It's none of your goddamn business who I am," he rumbled. He stood at least a head taller than Chuck.

He had not moved. Neither had Chuck, once he had come to a stop. "I'm making it my business," said Chuck, calmly deleting the profane use of the Lord's name.

By this time it had apparently registered on Zack that a question had been addressed to him. "This is Tony," said Zack, his voice thick. "He's my friend."

Chuck raised an eyebrow. "Is he now?"

"Uh huh."

Now Zack was not exactly what one would call an honor

student, but at the moment he sounded almost brainless, even by his own standards. It was as if Zack were talking through a wall, or from another dimension.

Chuck had already figured out what was happening. He didn't like it—not at all.

"Zack," and his voice was low and dangerous, "did this man give you something? What is it? Is it Snap? Is that it?"

The man that Zack had identified as Tony had clearly had enough. "Nobody asked you, jockstrap, it's none of your business—and you're going to regret you stuck your nose into this."

He grabbed for Chuck.

When Chuck had fought off, and humiliated, the bus driver, he had used a technique called *Ude-mochi-tekubi-kime*, or one-arm grasp, wrist lock. It, and moves similar to it, had been developed because in old Japan, one would perform a kneeling bow as a sign of greeting and respect to another individual if one were visiting the latter's home. This, however, was something that could disguise an intended attack, and so the *Suwari-waza*, the kneeling techniques, had been provided for those sorts of circumstances.

This time, however, Chuck was not kneeling. This time he had the full mobility to put an attacker's aggressiveness to work against the attacker.

But mercy. Always display mercy, and do the absolute minimum needed to halt the attack. That was all.

Tony came in quickly, and swung a vicious right cross toward Chuck. Chuck anticipated the move and backed up, quickly and surefootedly. It threw his attacker off balance and as his arm swept past, Chuck caught it and turned quickly, swinging the arm down and around. Tony left his feet, half-somersaulted through the air and slammed to the asphalt of the parking lot.

He lay there stunned for a moment, and Chuck went quickly to Zack. He looked deeply into his eyes, tried to find some hint of the young man's mind in there. "Zack, get out of here," he ordered. "Get a policeman. Get to a hospital."

Zack stared at him blankly, seemingly unconscious on his feet.

Something alerted Chuck, a footfall, something, and he turned quickly back toward Tony. The man now had a knife in his right hand. Chuck shoved Zack back, out of the way.

Tony clearly had experience using a knife, and he flipped it from his right hand to his left in an effort to confuse. Chuck ignored the knife hand, instead focused on the entire attacker, not allowing his attention to be diverted. When the man attacked, it would be with the knife in his right hand. Chuck was certain of that, and he poised defensively, hands up, legs loose, and ready to pivot.

Tony flipped the knife back to his right hand and tensed. Chuck sensed it, knew it. By contrast he was limber, ready. No tension, and yet his movements were quick, sure, and whipcord fast as Tony charged him, swinging the knife around.

Chuck's arm came up as his body half-turned, avoiding the thrust of the knife. Then he caught the wrist in a grip of steel and twisted. Tony screamed, his arm bending impossibly, and the knife slipped from his suddenly nerveless fingers and clattered to the ground.

Chuck pivoted in place and hurled the attacker toward the darkened school building. Tony's head slammed into the brick and he slid to the ground, groaning, flexing his fingers.

Zack keeled over.

Immediately Chuck's attention was on Zack. It was a tactical risk—if Tony had a gun on him, Chuck might be opening himself to attack. But he was certain Tony did not—otherwise he would have used it already.

He shook Zack desperately, shouted in his face, "Come on! Zack! Come back to me!" He felt the young man slipping away, felt as if somehow he could just reach in and touch the boy's mind and just pull him back if Chuck could only figure out how. "Come on, Zack," and he shook him once more. "What did he do to you? What did he give you?"

There was the roar of a car engine and headlights lanced across the parking lot. Chuck's head snapped around as a low-slung, jet-black car roared up and swung around, the passenger door flying open. Tony half-staggered, half-leaped toward it and fell into the passenger side. The door slammed shut.

Chuck, with no time anymore, scooped Zack up and started to run, the boy feeling weightless in his arms.

The wheels of the car spun for a moment and then it barreled toward Chuck.

Not too far away was a brick fence that demarcated the edge of the parking lot. It had been erected at the insistence of neighbors who were concerned that drunk students might come zipping through the parking lot, lose control, and wind up crashing through their backyards. The fence was six feet high and could withstand anything short of a Sherman tank.

Chuck ran for it now, his sneakered feet pounding on the pavement.

The car was bearing down on him. Like a deer caught in the oncoming lights of a truck on a highway, Chuck saw his shadow up ahead of him, framed in the headlights of the night-black car.

His thoughts scrambled frantically, fearfully. What the hell had he gotten himself involved in? What was happening?

The fence was still yards away and the car was—how close? He risked a glance behind him and saw that it was only a couple feet behind, about to run them down.

Chuck leaped to the right, almost flying through the air. He landed completely wrong, though, because he was trying to make sure he didn't land on the insensate Zack. His elbows ripped against the asphalt, and he felt a jolt of pain that went through his shoulders and, it seemed, out the back of his head.

He staggered to his feet, still clutching Zack, and ran again for the fence. Behind him the car screeched around and came toward them again.

STOP! his mind screamed.

And suddenly the car ripped to a halt, gears grinding in metallic protest, as if the stick had suddenly been slammed into park. The engine died, the ignition shut down.

From within the car, Chuck heard loud profanities, but he didn't pay any attention or question his good fortune— or perhaps the will of God. Whatever it was, it gave him the time he needed. He made it to the fence, staggering, for he had also torn up his knees when he fell. He shoved Zack up so that the young man was hanging half-over the fence and then leaped up after him, catching the edge with his fingertips and easily pulling himself up.

A gunshot cracked over his head, and he yanked Zack over and down. They fell the six feet into a neatly trimmed backyard, crashing into some bushes.

There was a furious roaring and barking and a German shepherd, snapping angrily, charged toward them.

It got to within a foot of them, and then Chuck, in no mood for any games, said angrily, "Shut up!"

The dog promptly stopped barking and stood there stunned, as if smacked across the face with a rolled-up newspaper that had a brick in it. Then the animal promptly turned and ran.

Chuck shook his head, gathered up Zack, and ran for the back of the house.

Chuck looked from one cop to the other in disbelief. "You're kidding."

They were in the living room of the Silversteins, the people into whose backyard Chuck had uninvitedly hurled himself. They were a polite, retired couple who seemed quite relieved (once they established that Chuck wasn't there to rob them) that Chuck had not been torn to shreds by their apparently vicious guard dog, Arnold.

"I've always had a way with dogs," Chuck had said which was his only explanation and indeed the only one he knew. The police had dutifully been summoned, Zack loaded into an ambulance, and the police—

"You're kidding," Chuck said again. "What do you mean, 'No proof that anything happened.' Look at me!" and he held up his cut and abraded arms. "Do I look like I was at a church social. And the boy! High on Snap, I'm positive of it."

"You an expert on drugs, Mr. Simon?" asked one of the cops.

"I've been taught to know symptoms, to recognize them."

"How convenient."

Chuck's eyes narrowed. "Would you gentlemen know the drug itself if you saw it?"

"Yes, sir," said one of the cops. "But that's not—"

"No, that *is* the point," said Chuck, anticipating what was about to be said. "You're implying something that I don't think I appreciate in the least, and I think I want to talk to your boss. That would be Chief Slezak, wouldn't it?"

"Yes, sir."

"Is he available?"

"Tomorrow, sir, during regular business hours, at the station."

"Fine." Chuck rose, and looked from one cop to the other. "You have my statement," he said tightly. "Unless there's something else . . . like, if you want to arrest me for almost being killed."

"No, sir, we're not going to arrest you."

The last word, unspoken, hung in the air: *Yet.*

"I don't suppose you gentlemen want to offer me a ride home."

"Against procedure, sir."

"Uh huh." He headed for the door and stopped only when one of the cops said, "Sir . . ."

He turned slowly.

The cop was looking at him through half-lidded eyes. "Don't leave town."

The threat was there, also unspoken: *Because you're a suspect in something, and we'll arrest you if you try to leave.*

"I wouldn't dream of it," said Chuck, and he walked out the door barely containing his anger.

The three men met on a deserted street corner.

Quint looked from one to the other. "Did you see any real proof?" he said.

"Proof of the aikido, all right," said Tony, still rubbing

his sore arm. "But no TK. Not for sure. Although he didn't need TK to almost score a TKO."

"He stalled out the car," said the other man who had been driving the dark car that was parked nearby.

"Are you sure, Jeffries?" demanded Quint.

The man he'd called Jeffries said with certainty, "It had to be him. All of a sudden the car's in park, the ignition key is shut off. Until he was clear, I couldn't even turn the key. It was like it was locked."

"That's not for sure," said Tony. "These models, sometimes the ignition freezes up on its own."

"Right, and the stick moves by itself too," sniffed Jeffries.

"It could have been bumped," Quint said in that whisper of his. "In the excitement. It's possible."

"This is all bullshit," snapped Jeffries. "If you think the guy's a TK, drag him in and run him through the wringer. Who needs all this shit?"

"Are you questioning orders?" Quint asked with silky menace.

Jeffries stood there a moment and then the point of his chin dropped to his chest. "I just think it's a pain in the ass, that's all."

"We do what's necessary," said Quint. "And we need concrete proof. These things can't be forced out in testing labs. They have to come out naturally, under stress. The conditions must be right."

"Great. So what's the next step?"

Quint told them.

Jeffries nodded slowly, not liking it particularly. "Why her?"

"Because she's shown interest in Simon. We have our sources keeping us apprised. We wait until an appropriate moment, and then we do it."

"And what if he catches on?" said Jeffries.

"He won't," said Quint.

"But what if—"

"He won't," repeated Quint with finality. "I'll be in touch with you at a later date with more information."

Tony and Jeffries headed back for their car. At the last moment Jeffries was struck by a thought and he turned to address it to Quint.

The dark man had vanished.

"I hate when he pulls that shit," said Tony.

"Yeah, well, whaddaya expect from a guy who wears sunglasses at night," retorted Jeffries. "Come on, 'drug pusher.' Let's get out of here."

5

If Chuck had been slow to believe what he was being confronted with the previous night, he was simply incredulous this day.

He had skipped the lunch period to shoot over to the police station, which was only three blocks away from the school. He left his newly repaired car, an eight-year-old two-door that he kept forgetting the make of, but knew that it was light blue, parked in front of the police station. Moments later he had been inside, asking to see the police chief, and after some hemming and hawing was brought in.

Slezak sat behind his desk and rose to shake Chuck's hand. But the moment Chuck came into contact with him, he could not shake the feeling that something was wrong. Not flat out malevolence, as he had sensed from the men yesterday. This was instead discomfort, uncertainty.

"Everything okay at home, Chief?" Chuck asked with genuine concern.

"Oh, fine! Fine," and Slezak laughed (nervously?) and gestured for Chuck to sit. Once the high school coach had made himself comfortable, he laid out the events of the previous night.

And Slezak shrugged expansively. "Nothing we can do," he said.

Chuck stared at him, appalled. "Chief, I don't understand," he said. "This is what your men said last night. Drug dealers, they're practically a thing of the past. What is some guy—some guys, excuse me—doing in a parking lot out here in Ohio, for pity's sake, selling drugs to a high school senior? It doesn't make sense."

"Did you actually see a transaction made?" Slezak's eyes narrowed.

"No. No, I didn't *see* anything, except for a young man who I'm certain was blitzed on Snap."

"You're familiar with what that looks like?"

Chuck's lips thinned as he said, "That's the same line of questioning your men took with me last night. They practically implied that I had given him the stuff in the first place."

Slezak looked at him askance. "My men implied that? I find that hard to believe."

"Well, I found it hard to believe too. Now what I want to know is when you're going to arrest these dealers?"

"We have only your word that they exist."

Chuck couldn't believe it. He almost rose up out of his chair, trying to keep his growing anger in check. Anger was not the way; a raised fist would only lead to a raised fist in return. "My word," he said, "is my word under God. I do not make false accusations, or bear false witness. There were two men, one of whom I saw, one of whom I did not see. They messed with a young man's head and could possibly have cost him his life. They tried to kill me. That is my word, and if it is insufficient for you, then perhaps I'll have to go to authorities for whom my word is good enough."

Their gazes locked across the desk, and then, his face

impassive, Slezak reached for a sheet of paper. He wet the end of a pencil with his tongue and then said evenly, "You want to describe them to me?"

Chuck described the knife man as best he could. It had been dark, and dressed in black as he was, he had seemed almost a fleeting shadow. Chuck wasn't especially thrilled with the seemingly nebulous description that he was forced to provide, but Slezak kept nodding and clucking his tongue as he dutifully took it all down. He looked up. "And the other man? And how about the car?"

"Never saw the driver," admitted Chuck. "Car was black, low-slung—I'm not real good with models. Fast, pretty fast, seemed almost new."

Slezak continued to nod, then put down his pencil. "All right," he said. "We'll put out an APB. That's an All Points Bulletin," he added, apparently proud of his ability to toss around lingo he'd probably picked up from TV. "If he's out there, we'll bring him in."

"He's out there," said Chuck. "They both are."

"Then we'll find them," said Slezak.

But Chuck still could not shake the feeling that something was being left unsaid. Something very serious. And he also couldn't stop thinking that Slezak intended to be exactly zero help.

Why? Why would the police not want to cooperate?

It was a question that whirled about in Chuck's head as he walked back out to his car. He couldn't get over it. Something, something was definitely not right. Something was out of kilter.

He tried to open the curbside car door and it banged against the curb, as if the curb had been raised in his absence. Or the car had shrunk.

He looked down and saw two flats on the passenger side. Both tires had holes in them, as if they'd been gouged with an ice pick. He ran around to the other side and found the other two tires flat as well.

From a distance away, there was a screech. He looked up and there, at the end of the street, was the black car from the night before. It spun around the corner at high speed, heading away from him, and tore off down a side road.

Chuck felt a wave of fright wash over him and he let it sweep through him and then out. As he did, his mind raced.

They had waited there. They had sat there until he'd come out, to make sure he saw it and make sure he knew who had done it. It was a warning, a threat. *Stay the hell out of our business,* it said. *Today tires. Tomorrow your lungs.*

Chuck did not take well to threats. Not well at all.

"Can you give me a lift to the hospital?" he asked Linda.

She looked up from her desk in surprise. She was just setting up for her next class, and could see immediately that something was wrong with Chuck. Usually he was the most calm, even-tempered, and even-keeled person she knew. Now, though, there was something very unsettled, even unsettling, about him.

"Are you feeling all right?" she asked him.

"It's not for me," he replied. "I want to go see Zack."

"Ooohh, right," she said. "But I can't take you right now."

"No, of course not," he said with uncharacteristic impatience. He made a visible effort to calm down and regain his poise. He forced a smile, his customary affability not coming easily. "After school is fine."

"Okay then." She paused, her eyebrows knit. "Why not just take your car? I saw you drive it in today."

"Four flats. I had to call to have it towed back to the service station. It'll be ready this afternoon."

Linda was not stupid, not remotely. She knew you didn't get four flats just by ill luck. "Who would do that?" she said.

"That's what Zack is going to tell us."

But by the time they got to the hospital, Zack wasn't there.

Chuck was appalled, and after making enough of a fuss, he finally convinced the nurses on-duty to bring down the attending physician for him to talk to. It was a Doctor Scully who was indicating by body posture—arms tightly folded, impatient look in his eyes—that he clearly had more important things to do.

He regarded the two teachers suspiciously, a clipboard pressed firmly under his arm. "Neither of you are family members?" he said.

"No, we're his teachers," Chuck told him.

Dr. Scully shrugged. "The details of the case are confidential. I'm sorry. Now I have rounds to make."

"Doctor . . ." Linda began.

But Scully wasn't listening as he started to turn and walk away.

"Hold it," said Chuck.

Scully froze.

He couldn't understand it. Suddenly, totally inexplicably, his legs had become immobile, rooted to the spot.

Chuck was walking around to face him, but Scully wasn't paying attention. He was trying to move his feet. For a horrifying moment he thought that perhaps he was having a stroke.

"Now listen," Chuck was saying, and Scully looked up in confusion. He had momentarily forgotten the teachers were there. "I've almost been killed for this kid—cars have tried to run me down, a man tried to knife me. My tires got slashed; that'll run me over six hundred dollars to replace. I think he was high on Snap. And I think I'm entitled to know for sure.''

Scully still couldn't get his legs to function, and he quickly realized he wasn't going to be able to attend to them until he got these idiot teachers out of his thinning hair. ''Look,'' said Scully urgently, ''his parents took him home. That's their right. They wanted to attend to him, and once we'd gotten the stuff out of his system—''

''So it was drugs of some sort,'' Linda said, walking up next to Chuck.

''*Yes*, all right?'' said Scully, at his wit's end. His legs were tingling. Maybe it was a heart attack. ''I'm sure it was Snap. I haven't seen it in action since I started residency in LeQuier, but I remember enough of my time in L.A. to know what it's like. Now will you people please move on? I'm having some problems here!''

''Fine, thank you,'' and Chuck took Linda by the elbow. ''C'mon, let's go,'' he said, and he practically pulled her off her feet as they hurried out of the hospital.

Scully, in the meantime, was desperately shouting for a nurse. But as the duty nurse ran up, Scully suddenly stumbled forward. The nurse stood there as Scully experimentally flexed his legs in confusion. ''What's wrong, Doctor?'' she asked.

He looked up at her, perplexed. ''Nothing.''

Zack's parents clearly did not want to cooperate any more than the doctor had. Perhaps less.

It was clear from the build of Zack's father where the boy got his football prowess from. The guy was immense with a head, comparatively speaking, the size of a thimble.

He held the door only half open, but what Chuck could make out of him was more than impressive.

"Sir," Chuck said, "we really have to talk to Zack."

"He's not seeing anyone," rumbled the father.

"Mr. Jordan," Linda said, "you don't understand. Coach here risked his life to save your boy. I really think that entitles us to a few minutes of his time."

"It entitles you to my thanks, but that's about it," said Jordan.

Chuck spoke as soothingly as he could. "Mr. Jordan," he said softly, "I know you're very uncomfortable about Zack's problem."

"Got no problem," said Jordan.

"Sir, as rare as drug use is nowadays, it still remains a—"

"No boy of mine is a drughead!" snapped Jordan.

The conversation was clearly not going well. Not only that, but Chuck would have almost been inclined to agree with Jordan. Not only were drugs hard, virtually impossible, to come by, particularly in small cities like LeQuier, but Zack had always been something of a straight arrow. This entire drug business had come up very abruptly, with very nasty results.

Jordan, meantime, was starting to slam the door in Chuck's face.

Chuck placed one hand against the door and, to Jordan's amazement, the angry father wasn't able to push it closed any further. Even Linda was impressed—Chuck was muscular, well-built—but he didn't appear to have anything resembling the sort of muscle power needed to thwart the aims of the walking land mass known as Mr. Jordan.

"He talks to me," said Chuck, "or he talks to the police."

It was something of a bluff, because Chuck was sure

that if the police were going to talk to Zack, they would have already. The fact that they hadn't, concerned him not a little.

Jordan appeared to be considering the threat, and then slowly he stepped aside and Chuck swung the door open. Jordan held up a hand, fingers spread. "Five minutes," he said. "He's upstairs. Second door on the right."

Moments later the teachers were standing in front of a door with signs on it that read KEEP OUT and DANGER: RADIATION. Chuck rapped on the door and, when he heard a grunt from inside, took that as an okay to enter and walked in, Linda right behind him.

Zack lay on his bed, wearing a faded blue sweat suit, his fingers laced behind his head. He was staring up at the ceiling.

Linda sat down nearby, Chuck elected to stand. "Zack," he said quietly. "How you feeling?"

Zack shrugged.

"Zack, we don't have a lot of time," Linda said, with a significant glance in the direction of the stairs. They could practically sense Mr. Jordan at the foot of the stairs, pacing and watching the seconds pass. "We have to know where you got the Snap."

Zack shrugged.

"It's important, Zack," Chuck prompted.

This time Chuck shrugged along with Zack, anticipating. He glanced at Linda with a "What now?" kind of look.

Linda's mouth twitched in thought for a moment. Then she walked over to Zack, sat down next to him, and to Chuck's astonishment, grabbed Zack fiercely by the front of his shirt. It also forced actual surprise to register on Zack's face.

"Now listen, you little snot," said Linda tightly, "People have gone out on a limb for you. People have risked their lives for you, and if you insist on trying to lie there like a vegged-out zombie, I'm going to remove your genitals and shove them down your throat. Do we understand each other?''

Zack nodded mutely, the blood drained from his face.

Linda released him and he plopped backwards. Chuck didn't know what to say. Fortunately, at that moment he didn't have to say anything.

''These two guys,'' Zack whispered, ''they came up to me a couple weeks ago. Said it was stuff that would boost my running game. You said my running game needs work, Coach.''

''Oh God, Zack, not like that,'' moaned Chuck.

''Said it would make me faster,'' said Zack. ''Said it was experimental, they'd pay me to try it. They did. I did. Now I feel like I can't live without the stuff.''

''You're going to feel like that for a while longer,'' said Chuck. ''It affects you that way. You just have to hang tough for a week or so, enough to let your system get it out of you. Otherwise it could kill you, Zack. Or worse.''

Zack frowned. ''Worse?''

''Impotence.''

Zack's mouth moved but no words came out at first. ''They . . . they never said that.''

''Well, it's not one of your better selling points,'' said Chuck. ''Look, Zack—these guys. Did they always contact you? How did you get more of it?''

''There was a number I could call. Someone always there, and I'd tell them I'd need it, and they'd say where they'd meet me. Never asked for money, I never had to show them my card. Like they're just giving me the stuff for free.''

That was the puzzling thing for Chuck. Because of the

cards, drug dealing had become extremely difficult. Absolutely everything was traceable. Only in the major cities, where drugs could be used for barter (most prostitutes, for example, were also addicts, and their suppliers also their "business managers"), did any sort of dealing still thrive. Drug dealers were in business to make money, not give the stuff away.

But that was what these guys were doing, if Zack could be believed. And Chuck had a feeling he could be. He was too scared, and too out of it, to be up to much prevarication.

"All right, Zack," said Chuck. "Here's what I want you to do. Call the number. Tell them you want to see them tonight, that you need another hit. Get the time and place. We'll do the rest."

Linda shot him a look that said *We?*

Zack looked from Chuck to Linda. Linda noticed and put on her fierce expression with utter conviction. Without another word Zack reached over and picked up the phone. As he dialed, Chuck made a mental note of the phone number.

Zack was silent for a long moment, and for a few seconds Chuck was certain that the dealers had blown town. But no, he heard a faint murmur on the other end, and Zack was saying, hoarsely, "It's me. I need to see you."

He paused, nodded, and then he looked up.

Chuck glanced at his watch. The whole conversation couldn't have taken more than ten seconds.

"They said," Zack continued quickly, as if anxious to wash his hands of the whole thing, "they said tonight, at seven, at the corner of Vine and Rosedale."

"Okay," smiled Chuck. "Okay, Zack. You've done the right thing. We're going to call the police. We're going to nail them. And they won't be able to hurt you or anyone else again."

"I've run that phone number you gave me through the computer," said Slezak over the phone, "and gotten nothing on it. It could be a car phone. Could be anything. Either way we can't trace it."

"Now look, Chief," Chuck said, gripping the phone more tightly. "These guys are—"

"Relax, Coach," came the slow reply, "because we won't have to find them. We'll be there at the corner of Vine and Rosedale, waiting. One of our undercover men will be disguised as Zack—should be easy enough, we got at least two guys who are that type. And when the dealers show up with the Snap in their possession, we got them cold. Just having the stuff is enough to send you away for ten years."

"All right," said Chuck, "and what do I do?"

"Nothing. You've done everything you should. The rest is our job. Go out for the evening. Have a good time. You owe it to yourself. I'm asking you to stay away from where the arrest is going to go down, because I really don't want to put any civilians at risk. By tomorrow morning these guy's asses will be on the griddle, and you'll have helped put them there."

Chuck smiled at that and nodded. "Okay, then," he said. "If you're sure."

"Positive."

Before Chuck could say anything further, Slezak hung up. But really, there wasn't anything more to say.

Chuck turned to where Linda was leaning against the hood of her car. "Well?" she said.

He spread his hands wide. "It is in the capable hands of the police," he said.

He walked over toward Linda and then stopped, looking at her with mock trepidation. "I dunno, maybe I should be careful around you," he said. "Wouldn't want to swallow my genitals or anything."

She laughed at that and, as she did so, flushed slightly, which Chuck was pleased to see. "I was just helping to do nice cop, tough cop."

"It sounded more like nice cop, psychotic cop."

"Whatever works," she shrugged.

"You really scared Zack."

"But did I scare you?"

He raised an eyebrow. "I don't scare easily."

"You've been scared to go out with me."

There was definite challenge in her voice, and his eyebrow arched higher. "Oh, really."

"Yes, really. Hiding behind the shadow of your ex-wife, pining away for her. It's embarrassing. I'm embarrassed for you, when you could be going out with a great woman like me, and instead you're being faithful to a woman who walked out on you."

He grimaced. "Does make me sound like the prize chump of the year, doesn't it."

"Yeah, a little."

"Okay then," he said with sudden conviction. "Tonight. I'll pick you up at seven, how's that?"

"Without your car?"

"You're going to drive me over to the service station right now. It's only ten minutes away."

"Well, that's damned nice of me," she said.

"I thought so."

They hopped in the car and took off, and Linda glanced over at Chuck. He looked very relaxed, even—what? Fulfilled? "You seemed really driven to do something about

Zack. You always had some sort of emotional attachment to him?''

Chuck shrugged. "It's not that so much, really."

"Then what?"

"It's called 'bearing witness.' If I see something that I know is wrong, I can't pretend that it doesn't exist. I have to do something about it. It's a kind of religious thing."

"Oh." She paused. "I think that's nice."

"So do I."

Chuck checked himself out in the mirror once more and then smiled at himself. Not bad, he thought. Not too shabby. His crisp blue skirt had the top two buttons stylishly undone, and he shrugged on his white blazer that nicely complemented his white slacks. No, not too bad at all. His first serious date since the divorce, and it was with a woman who tanned herself all over.

Not that he would see that, of course. Not on a first date. Oh, he'd known Linda for some time, but this was the first time they'd gone out. It wouldn't be appropriate for him to start seriously coming on with her until they knew—

He paused. "What if she starts with me?" he said out loud to the empty bedroom. It wasn't impossible, after all. What would he do then?

Just be natural and calm. That was all. Don't fight whatever direction the evening might take. A nice dinner out was all that was planned, and maybe a movie. A nice, old-fashioned evening in LeQuier.

He left his house, not knowing that he would never see it again, hopped in his car and headed off for his date.

6

AFTER CHIEF SLEZAK got off the phone with Chuck, he continued to do routine paperwork and chat animatedly with his subordinates. And when the clock was pushing six, he rolled back his chair, went out to the parking lot and drove home. He planned, of course, to spend the rest of the evening in. Naturally, as per instructions, he intended to do nothing about Chuck's concerns. Just as he had never sent out the APB, or even filed the complaint reports.

Some time later he was relaxing at home, his feet up, a beer in his hand, his wife in the kitchen, a quiz show on the tube. It was all very nice, and he was more than a little put out when his private line rang. It was, of course, the fire chief, calling to inform Slezak of the massive explosion that had occurred, and the connected fatalities. Slezak went white when he heard what had happened and who was involved, and for the first time began to question whether a five thousand credit extension was worth selling your soul for.

Chuck enjoyed driving, especially in the evening. The ride felt particularly smooth, and he tried to put as good a face

on the tire mishap as he could. The car needed new tires
anyway, he decided. Probably the best thing that could
have happened. Definitely was hugging the road a lot better. Besides, he never really spent money on much of anything anyway. So what if it was six hundred dollars? Big
deal. He could handle it.

Nothing wrong with showing Linda a smooth ride.

He spotted her street coming up, signaled, and made a
leisurely right turn. Her small house was up three and on
the right—

And his head began to split.

He slammed on the brakes, his mind assaulted, and his
head slammed forward and hit the steering wheel. He sat
up, dazed, and peered with blurred vision at the house.

It seemed normal. It seemed all right. But something,
something was definitely wrong. He didn't know what,
and he didn't know how he knew, but something had happened.

He leaped out of the car, leaving the engine running,
and dashed toward the house. It was a small, two-floor
cape, and the lights were on. In front of it were assorted
freestanding shrubberies that Linda had carefully sculpted
herself into the shapes of animals.

He dashed up the flagstone walkway, shouting Linda's
name.

The front door open, and Linda was not the one standing there.

Chuck froze for a split instant.

It was Tony. Tony the drug dealer.

Chuck glanced at his watch. Seven o'clock. Tony should
have been across town.

But Tony was grinning. "You thought you were going
to pull something, didn't you, Coach? Should've known

better than to fuck with us, pal. You and your girlfriend both.''

"What have you done with her?!" shouted Chuck, and he started towards Tony. "Where is she?!"

Tony was standing there, the picture of calm, and seconds later it became evident why.

From behind the shrubs, darkly clad men came leaping out. Six of them, wielding knives and clubs.

Again, no guns. They weren't out to kill him. Or maybe they were, and wanted it to be slow.

Chuck barely had time to clear his mind before they charged him.

They attacked simultaneously, from all sides. Chuck had no time for subtlety. He grabbed the nearest one as his assailant swung a club at him, sidestepping and twisting in perfect combination, hurling the one attacker into another. He sidestepped a third, slammed his foot back into the man's knee, and now the fourth was coming in with the knife. Chuck blocked, but the knife man twisted away before Chuck could get a grip on him.

A fist slammed into the back of Chuck's head and he went down, shoulder rolled, and started to scramble to his feet just as he saw a well-placed kick coming at his face. He ducked while swinging his arm up, knocking the attacker onto his back. He started to get back up and Chuck grabbed the attacker and crunched his head down into the ground.

Something warned Chuck at the last second and he leaped out of the way as a knife slammed down where he'd been. He got to his feet as three of them were coming at him. Together they lunged, and Chuck backpedaled, grabbing the wrist of the nearest one and twisting it. He hated to do it, but this was life and death. He had to defend himself, and he had to get to Linda. The wrist broke and the man shrieked in pain, dropping the knife.

The second of the three swung a club down. Chuck blocked with one hand, and with the other pushed the man's arm back. It was fast, hard, and vicious and the man screamed as he went down backward with a dislocated shoulder.

But before Chuck could move he was broadsided across the knees, and he went down. He tried to roll out from under his attacker but another was on top of him, and then a third. He struggled furiously, grabbing at joints, trying to get a hold, but they had him pinned. Within seconds he was hoisted off the ground, two men were holding his hands, two others his feet. He saw two men rolling on the ground in agony, but took small comfort in that.

"Together!" Tony was shouting. "Now!"

And Chuck was sailing through the air, to finally land hard in the street. He rolled, the asphalt ripping his nice white clothes, tearing up his skin.

He clambered to his feet and Tony was running from the house, shouting something. "Kiss your girlfriend goodbye!" he was shouting. That was it. That was—

The house exploded.

A fireball rocketed skyward, the air crackling, and Chuck's screams were drowned out as a second explosion ripped through the air. Timber blew sky-high, plummeted to the ground blocks away, and fried grass, and all around Chuck it seemed like a blast furnace. Fragments of house flew all over—

She was in there, Chuck's mind screamed, *she was in there. I started this and they finished it and she's dead and it's my fault.*

And something inside of Chuck's head turned over, like

a light clicking on, or an engine being jump started. A psychic battery charged, a connection was made.

Something that had always been there, that he had known deep down he was capable of, but he had always ascribed to luck or chance or blind providence. He did not want to be different. Or odd. Or a freak.

Neighbors were running out from the houses now, and Chuck saw the men running off, heading toward a large van that he hadn't spotted before. And Tony was leaping into a different car.

They were running from the fire. They were afraid of the fire. They had consigned Linda to it, but they were afraid.

The fires. The pit.

And somewhere inside, Chuck Simon, the Quaker, snapped.

"Burn," he said.

The men didn't know what was happening. All they knew was that suddenly, one by one, they were being lifted off their feet, utterly helpless, as if in the grip of a giant fist.

Chuck turned, the fire of the house reflected in his wild eyes, and again he said "Burn," like the death-knell of a soul.

They hurtled through the air, screaming and pinwheeling their arms, thrashing their legs. And they sailed straight into the inferno of the house, the flame licking their bodies to welcome them.

Neighbors screamed in horror, shouting, and running about like headless chickens. Also screaming was Chuck's soul, Chuck's beliefs and philosophies.

Love humanity. Be at peace with nature.

But how? How could you be at peace with a nature

befouled? How could you love humanity that could do—this?

And by acting as one of them, he was becoming one of them, and he simply didn't care.

Tony stopped just outside his car, and saw the other men hurled to their deaths. He stared at Chuck, who was standing there, riveted, like primitive man gazing at the frightening horrors that lay within the forest.

Tony leaped into his car, no longer caring about the mission. Provoke him, he had been ordered. Push the TK. See if it will manifest.

Well, he had pushed, all right. And it had manifested into the hideous deaths of six men. With a seventh quite possibly in the offing.

But Simon seemed to have forgotten about him.

He slammed his foot on the gas and roared toward Chuck.

Chuck saw him coming at the last moment and reached out with his mind, envisioned the brake pedal, and slammed it down.

The car halted and Tony hurled forward, smashing his head into the windshield. A crack ribboned across it and Tony, grasping at the door handle, fell out of the car, blood welling up from the wound in his forehead.

He yanked the gun out of his shoulder holster as Chuck advanced on him, silhouetted against the evening sky that was alive with flame and heat. He seemed like a berserk god.

Tony brought the gun around and Chuck's mind yanked the gun away with such force that Tony's trigger finger went with it. The gun hurtled through the air to land in the burning house, and Tony vaguely heard the repeated explosions of the bullets in the clip being detonated by the heat. But he wasn't paying attention, instead occupied with the blood that was pumping from his maimed hand.

Chuck advanced on him, and in a voice like death, he said, "Simon says stand."

Tony was yanked to his feet by nothing.

"Simon says die."

He reached out, the invisible fist clamping on Tony's chest. With horrifying ease he crushed Tony's vitals; lungs and heart collapsed in on themselves, blood vessels rupturing, brain crumbling and turning into a hideous mass that oozed out of Tony's ears. And he pulped him and pummeled him long after the body had lost the ability to feel anything—pain or sorrow or happiness or anything, and he was just dead, that's all. Just dead, and it wouldn't bring Linda back, and it wouldn't bring Chuck's soul back or mind back or—

"CHUCK!"

The scream had come from behind him.

It was Linda.

He turned and saw her car pulling up and she leaped out of it, frantic and hysterical. She was shouting something about getting the call from Chuck to meet him at his place, and when she'd got there he hadn't been there and what was happening and—

Then he blacked out.

7

JEFFRIES, THE FORMER partner of the late Tony, slowly ran the tape back for what seemed the umpteenth time.

He had gotten everything, every moment of the slaughter, on videotape. He had been across the street, in the house they had taken over for the duration, tape machine whirring. Every desperate gesture and agonized expression of the men was etched on the tape. Every howl and scream for help was part of the sound recording. And not only that. It was forever inscribed into Jeffries' agonized memory.

He ran it back and watched it again, and still couldn't believe it.

They had not expected it, not anticipated it at all. Simon was supposed to be a Quaker. A pacifist. This—this was straight out of a horror film. Jeffries freeze-framed it, staring again in disbelief at the men floating in the air. One of them was already being thrust headfirst into the fire. He found himself looking for strings somewhere that might be supporting them, insane as it sounded. But was the idea of strings any more insane than the truth?

He ran it forward, watched Tony's body both implode and explode, as if his insides had come to life and tried for liberation. From this angle he couldn't make out Simon's face, but he heard the voice.

Simon says.

A child's game. Simon says you do this, you do this. Simon says you live, you live. Simon says your body crumbles up into a throbbing mass of tissue, then that's what happens, too. That's the game. That's the rule.

They had not expected this at all. They had assumed that he would levitate somehow, to try and get above the fire. Or perhaps use the TK to actually extinguish the fire. Or enter it, mentally pushing back the flames to provide safety for himself.

But not this. Obviously he had been certain that the girl was killed in the explosion. He had assumed that the men had decided to eliminate the girl and had gone about it with ruthless efficiency. Indeed, had that been their intention, he would have been correct. But they had not intended to kill her at all. That was why Jeffries had called, imitating Simon (and quite effectively, he had thought), informing her that his car had broken yet again and she was to come to his place. He'd even suggested a shortcut for her to take—a shortcut which, naturally, made sure that she would not accidentally drive past Simon who was on the way to her house.

He'd gone berserk, that was all. He had snapped. And seven men were dead.

A door opened and closed behind him. He glanced behind him and the dark man was there. "Quint," he said in a low voice. "You heard?"

Quint nodded.

"He's a Quaker," Jeffries said. "A goddamn Quaker."

Quint walked up to him and stood there silently for a long moment. "There's a story," he said slowly, "of how a burglar broke into the home of a Quaker, and was confronted by the home's owner, who was holding a large rifle. Since they were on a farm, rifles were commonplace, you see. And the burglar stood there, grinning at this Quaker, figuring the man wouldn't do anything. And the Quaker said, 'Brother, I would not hurt thee for all the world, but thou art standing where I am about to shoot.' ''

Jeffries stared at him. ''That's a real fine goddamn story, Quint,'' he said. ''What's the point of it?''

''The point is: Never underestimate the opposition,'' said Quint. ''Something to remember in future dealings with Simon.''

''Future dealings?'' and Jeffries' voice went up in anger and confusion. ''The only future dealings I want to have with this bastard are through the cross hairs of a scope. And you! This was your idea! If it weren't for you— *urrchhh!*''

His voice had abruptly halted, because Quint had quite calmly closed his gloved hand around Jeffries' throat.

''Now listen to me carefully,'' said Quint. ''You do as I tell you, when I tell you. You do not question. You think I give a damn about a handful of men? Especially when we can gain something like Simon?'' He squeezed tighter, and Jeffries' face started to turn blue. ''There's an old saying: You can't make an omelette without breaking a few eggs. Ever hear it?''

Jeffries tried to nod.

''It's a good saying,'' and Quint's ominous voice was low and whispered. He released his hold on Jeffries, and the smaller man staggered back gasping for air. He tried to pull together some sort of response, but Quint was already ignoring him.

Instead he sat down in front of the set.

''Play it,'' he said.

He sat back, steepling his fingers, and watched intently as Jeffries rewound the tape and started it over again.

He watched the physical assault on Simon, followed by the mental assault. He watched the men hurling to their deaths, the explosive termination of Tony.

And for the first time since Jeffries had met Quint, Jeffries saw something that chilled him more than anything ever had before.

Quint smiled.

8

LINDA SAT SHIVERING in the office of Chief Slezak. It wasn't particularly cold, but icy fingers played across her spine and she trembled under their touch. She was sipping her second cup of black coffee, and it still wasn't removing the chill from her.

Slezak sat across from her, silent as he had been for some time now.

Finally she looked him in the eye. "Can I see him?" she asked, her voice barely above a whisper.

"I'm not sure that's wise," Slezak said.

"I'm not either. But I want to. I have to."

He paused, trying to find a delicate phrase. "It's none of my business, Miss Hollaway, but were you and Coach Simon, uhm . . ." His voice trailed off, but the intent of the question was clear.

She shook her head. "Friends, chief. Just . . . just friends." She looked down at her coffee and said more softly, "Just friends."

"It's difficult for us to determine his state of mind right now," said Slezak. "He's just staring off into space. It's like he's gone into shock. The reports I've heard, the things the witnesses said—everything from some sort of psychic power to aliens coming down with anti-gravity rays. But it all comes back to the Coach.''

"Yes, it does, doesn't it," she said.

She had not told the police what she had seen. How she had pulled up just in time to witness the demise of a man fitting the description Chuck had given her of one of the drug dealers. Chuck had been standing there, arms outstretched, and he had closed his fists, and the man had just seemed to—

She closed her eyes against the memory, unable to blot it from her mind's eye.

"Alien gravity rays," she said wonderingly. Why was that easier to deal with than the truth? Why was she hoping that, all of a sudden, flying saucers were going to drop from the skies and take responsibility for all that had happened.

"What I'm saying," Slezak started again, "is that if you do go in to see him . . . well, Miss, we can't guarantee your safety.''

She nodded. "I understand that.''

"Are you sure?''

"Yes.''

"Okay," and he opened a desk drawer and pulled out a form. He pushed it across the desk. "Then you won't mind signing this.''

She looked at it with mild interest. "A release form.''

"Insurance purposes. You understand. We don't want something to happen to you and then have you, well, go sue the city.''

"You mean something happening like that man Chuck crushed.''

There. She'd said it. She'd finally managed to get it out.

"That's right," Slezak said coldly.

"And you won't let me see Chuck unless I sign this.''

"That's right," he said again.

She pulled the paper toward her. "Give me a pen," she said.

Chuck sat alone at a table in the witness interrogation room. Since things were generally pretty quiet in LeQuier, it also served as the lunchroom and the poker room. Because of that it was usually filled with the steady chatter of cops talking or laughing or telling off-color jokes in between bites of their sandwiches.

Now, though, it was dead silent. Only Chuck was there, still wearing his ash-stained and ripped clothing. He stared off at nothing, his fingers neatly interlaced in front of him on the table, as if he were an attentive student in school.

There were no cops inside. No one wanted to risk the duty. They stood outside the door, occasionally peering in to make sure that Chuck was still there. No one wanted to look him in the eye, as if there were a demon hiding in there and might leap out if it noticed them.

Slezak walked up with Linda and gestured to the officers on duty that they should let her in. They looked at Linda with a mixture of morbid curiosity and fear. They had heard the witness reports too, and wondered if this attractive young woman would meet the same grisly demise that those other men, whoever they were, had.

Linda heard the door close behind her, a wordless vote of non-confidence. Chuck sat there, not seeming to have noticed her.

"Chuck?" she whispered.

No answer.

She went to him, forced herself to look him in the eyes. They were vacant, lifeless. If it hadn't been for the slow rising and falling of his chest, she might have thought he was dead.

"Chuck, say something."

Still no answer.

"Chuck, I want you to know . . . I saw what happened. And I'm . . . I'm not afraid of you."

Something seemed to stir in him, and slowly he looked up at her. He didn't quite meet her gaze, but there was some vague hint of animation in him.

"I know you wouldn't hurt anyone, Chuck. I mean—I know you did," she said, feeling like a tongue-tied idiot. "But that wasn't you. I mean—it was you, but you were upset, and you thought I'd been killed, and anyone might have done what you did. I mean, anyone who could just—"

Just what? Kill with the power of their mind alone? Just think someone dead and they were crushed like an over-ripe melon?

Who in hell was she kidding? There was no analogy for this, nothing to compare it to. This wasn't a man who had blown his temper and struck his wife and now was feeling guilty and contrite. It wasn't even someone who had gone berserk after a really, really bad day, grabbed up a rifle and started firing shots at people out of a window.

He had done something; something that came from within and been unleashed by thought alone. Something that was contrary to his very being, to his philosophies and beliefs. Something that, had he seen someone else do it, would have repelled and horrified him. But he himself had done it. How was he supposed to deal with that?

And how was she? Every time she looked at him, she realized, she would see his face as it had been mere hours ago: twisted and furious, seared with ash mixed with blood, a wildness in his eyes, his hair skewed and singed. . . .

And berserk. He had gone berserk.

Could it happen again? She would always wonder, always question. Could something she might say or do set him off, drive him over the edge again? Might he lash out again at someone? At her?

What could she say to him now? What could she possibly say? That she would stick by him, support him? What was she letting herself in for if she said that? Good God, when it came down to it, she really didn't know him all that well. Sure, she knew him from school, and he seemed like a fun and sexy guy. Outgoing, pleasant. But now she'd seen what she was capable of, and she sensed that any emotional attachment right now was more of a commitment to him than she was prepared to give.

By slow degrees, she had gone from completely supportive to completely afraid of what involvement with Chuck might entail. And she realized that she was simply not going to be able to deal with it.

"Chuck," she whispered, "I'm so sorry about everything that happened. And I hope that everything works out for you." She kissed him on the top of his head and then, her lips against his ear, she murmured, "God be with you."

She turned and hurried out of the room and out of his life.

He was alone now. Totally alone.

He had been aware of Linda's presence, as if it were a fast-fading dream. She had been there, and now she was gone, and that was all there was of her.

It was probably best for her. He had liked her, he really had. The depths of his affection for her had not been apparent to him until he had thought she had been killed.

Or was it just her? Would he have reacted the same if, say, it had been Zack's house that was blown up with Zack inside it. How much of it was his feeling of responsibility? After all, his belief that one cannot stand by and let something wrong go unchecked had supposedly led to her death. How could that be? How could a philosophy of benign intervention lead to evil ends?

It wasn't fair. It wasn't just. If you let evil go unattended, tragedy can result. But if you step in and try to stop evil, tragedy still can result. He knew that life wasn't fair, but that was ridiculous. Absurd. Unjust. How could there be a just God when such things could happen?

How could there be a God when things such as he had done could happen?

He would never be able to forget it. The inner horror and loathing of what he had done, he felt, had corrupted him beyond all hope of redemption. The Society of Friends? The Society of Murderers was more like it. He was the most vile of creatures, the most heinous of fiends. The Society of Fiends. There was a mirthless irony to that, and he felt a darkness growing in him.

Perhaps he should kill himself. Perhaps only his life could pay for what he had done to others.

But the others had been murdering parasites. They had preyed on Zack. They had attacked and tried to kill Chuck, and then Linda.

But Linda wasn't home. They must have known that. So was it a charade, and if so, for what insane purpose?

They had been villains with no regard for life. And Chuck was a Quaker, with the highest regard for life, but they had killed no one and their blood was on his hands.

His power. His ungodly power, that must have come straight from the bowels of hell, for certainly it could not have come from heaven. He was unclean. He had always known it, deep down. Always there had been impure thoughts in him, feelings that he had tried to deal with.

It is the way of the warrior, he had always told himself. Not to believe that you are perfect, but instead to believe that you are imperfect and to strive to overcome those imperfections. To strive for balance, the evil against the good. That is the way of the warrior: balance.

He was unbalanced.

Aikido was an art that combined with nature. But nature had deteriorated, was polluted by man. How could you be at one with nature and not be sullied by that same man-made taint?

Unclean. Unclean. The Biblical warning to be uttered when a leper was in the presence of healthy individuals.

He wanted to rip the skin from himself, or else consign his soul to the darkness it so richly deserved.

And he looked up.

He had not even seen the man come in. He stood there, clad in dark clothes, wearing sunglasses and a hat pulled down low.

"Mr. Simon," he said.

Chuck stared at him silently.

"My name is Quint," he said, and from the pocket of his coat he pulled out an ID billfold and tossed it to Chuck. Chuck caught it automatically and opened it without much interest.

He frowned.

The upper portion had a badge. The lower portion had a Card, similar to Chuck's and the other cards that were standard issue. But there were some differences. For one thing, this had a picture of Quint in the upper left hand corner, which meant that it was used for casual visual identification as well. The second thing was that, while every other card Chuck had ever seen was white, this one was gold. The third thing was that Quint's name did not appear on it, although Chuck's clearly read *"Charles An-*

thony Simon" across the middle. Instead of that, Quint's had a logo stamped in the middle. The logo, in blood red, read simply: THE COMPLEX.

"Have you heard of us?" asked Quint.

"Sure I've heard of you," said Chuck slowly. His voice sounded odd to him, and he realized it was the first time he'd used it in hours. "I've also heard of UFOs, the Loch Ness Monster, and—"

"Telekinesis?"

The word, spoken by Quint, hung there. Chuck said nothing.

"Mr. Simon," he said, his voice cool and detached, "you are doubtlessly very frightened right now. You have a power and don't know how to control it, or even if you can. We can help you."

There was no follow-up to that statement. Quint merely stood there, and finally Chuck could not resist. "How?"

"We can teach you how to control it."

"I don't want to control it. I want to get rid of it."

"All right."

There was a gun in Quint's hand. He walked over and lay it down in front of Chuck.

"Put it to your temple, squeeze the trigger," said Quint. "That is the only way you can eliminate the power you have."

Chuck stared at it. Then he picked it up. It felt heavier than he would have thought; the metal was cold in his grasp. He turned it over, stared down the muzzle. Death stared back at him, called to him, laughed at him.

"Just as your body has been trained to defend itself," Quint told him, "your mind can be trained to defend itself. Your power can be harnessed, used for good. For the good of your country. You can reattain inner peace by disciplining your power. Or," he observed, "you can skip training, skip all of that, and use the gun to decorate the walls with your brain. It's up to you."

Chuck said nothing.

"The Complex is the greatest intelligence gathering agency in the history of the United States," said Quint. "All others became obsolete when our charter was established. You can be a part of that. Or you can be part of the next paint job in this room."

Chuck looked up at him. "It won't bring those men back," he said.

"No. Look, Simon, right now you're afraid to live because of what you did. But you're afraid to die because it leaves too many questions unanswered, the most fundamental of which is—why do you have this power? Why would God give it to you if he intended you to use it for evil?"

"Maybe someone else gave it to me," said Chuck darkly.

"You'll never find out, will you, unless you try? And if you die now, the only thing of note that you've ever accomplished is the death of seven men. That leaves the scales tilted in a direction I don't think you like. If you give yourself the opportunity to use your powers for good, then you can even the scales again. Attain balance once more. Or, as I said," and he tapped the gun that Chuck was holding, "you can take the easy way out. The quick way. The coward's way. But whatever you're going to do, decide now. Because I have other things to attend to."

"The law—" Chuck began, "the charges against me—"

"What charges?" said Quint. "There are no charges."

"But only if I go with you."

"No," said Quint. "We don't work that way. I've made sure there are no charges—it was self-defense, after all.

But that's all. If you join us or don't join us, you still leave here with a clean slate.''

At that, Chuck laughed inwardly. There were stains on that slate that could never be expunged. Not by a coach at LeQuier High School, at any rate.

Not by the loose cannon that he had become.

Slowly he lay the gun down.

''Where do I sign on?'' he asked.

March 22, 2021

9

"Now concentrate."

Chuck held up the spoon and stared at it, his brow furrowing. His lips were drawn tightly back, and a thin sheen of perspiration formed on his forehead.

Slowly, as he grunted, the spoon began to bend.

Across the table from him sat Doctor Ferguson, a heavyset, bearded man who was perpetually making notes. Ferguson nodded in approval as, over five agonizing minutes, Chuck managed to bend the spoon—

Five degrees.

He dropped the spoon, finally, panting with exhaustion, and slumped back in the chair.

Ferguson picked up the spoon, turned it all around. Then he lay it down next to a protractor and started studying it.

"That's an improvement," said Chuck hopefully. "You used to use a microscope to measure the bends."

Ferguson looked up and said nothing, which was about standard for Ferguson.

"Am I free to go now?" asked Chuck. Ferguson gestured and Chuck, nodding, got up and left the small testing room.

Outside the usual haze hung over the sky, the air feeling thicker than usual. Chuck coughed as he looked up and wondered if there was anyplace in the United States—in the world, for that matter—where the air was crisp and clean, and your lungs could be stung with the briskness of the weather rather than with the pollutants.

The headquarters of the Complex was a truly majestic affair, with large, sleek buildings that were mostly glass. Had there been a sun capable of cutting through the cloud cover, it would have given a gorgeous reflection that might have been a hint of what architecture in heaven was like. It had taken Chuck about a week to really learn his way around, be able to pick out the living quarters from the testing quarters, the library from the eatery. *Everything except a gift shop*, he had thought.

He started walking across the grounds, through with testing for the day. Testing, training, that was all his life consisted of now, it seemed. He jammed his hands deep into the pockets of his jeans, the hood of his blue sweat-shirt pulled up over his head. It was unseasonably brisk and he wondered when summer might be coming.

"HEADS UP!"

The shout was unexpected and Chuck turned quickly, just in time to see a football headed straight at him. He didn't move but suddenly the football halted in mid-air.

Standing nearby was Quint. His arms were folded, and he was leaning against the base of a statue of former President Quayle. His sunglasses, as always, were in place, and Chuck found it disconcerting talking to someone when he could never make eye-contact with them.

The moment Chuck saw him, the football fell to the ground, bouncing noisily.

"Very good," said Quint. "That's the most TK ability you've shown in months."

Chuck looked down at his feet. He scratched at the beard he had begun growing three weeks ago, which was coming in surprisingly dark considering the blondness of his hair. "It's difficult to just—call it up consciously. Dr. Tyler calls it 'repressing.' "

Quint sighed. The Complex shrink he didn't exactly get along with all that well. "Dr. Tyler can call it all the names he wants," he said. "You're not going to be able to discipline your power until you can control it. Call it up at your command."

"It's difficult."

"So you've said." He held up a spoon, slightly bent, which Chuck recognized as one that he'd worked on last week. He flipped it to Chuck, who caught it.

"So tell me about your ex," said Quint.

Chuck was surprised. "My ex? You mean Anna?"

"Yes. How'd you two meet?"

"In a supermarket," and he cast his mind back and smiled. "She was looking all over for some item that was on sale—a brand of coffee—and she couldn't find it. The sales clerks all gave her blank stares, and she was getting really frustrated. And I found her a can, stuck behind some others. And she said to me—she had this really great voice, like she was always laughing even when she wasn't. Anyway, she said to me, 'I'm just terrible at shopping. I can never find anything.' And I told her that that was no problem for me, that I'd help her because I have a real . . . knack."

His voice trailed off and he looked at Quint. "My God," he said slowly, "even back then. That was my power manifesting, even back then, wasn't it."

"These things don't spring into existence overnight, Chuck," said Quint. "I think if you review your life, you'll be amazed at how many times, consciously and unconsciously, your power has acted in your behalf. It's a part of you, an extension of you. Not something to be afraid of. Any more than you should be afraid of your hand, since, if you twist it in just the right way, you can break somebody's wrist. Your power is on your side, if you'll let it be.'' And he inclined his head toward Chuck's open palm, where Chuck had been holding the spoon.

Chuck looked down at it. The spoon had been twisted into a delicate-looking ''A.'' He held it up in surprise.

''Wife's name was Anna, did you say?'' asked Quint, although of course he already knew the answer.

Chuck nodded numbly.

''Work on your balance,'' said Quint, ''and I think you'll be amazed what you can do.'' He turned and walked away, leaving Chuck alone.

10

DIMITRI PANSHIN STOOD on the pedestrian overpass, glancing down at the traffic that passed briskly beneath him on the highway. The breeze came up and whipped about his raincoat as a slow, gentle rain fell upon him from the skies over Washington, D.C. His hat was fur, real fur, the kind that was impossible to come by these days with the way the animal population had dwindled.

He looked at his watch and frowned. Where the devil was Smithers? He should have been here by now, and every minute that he was overdue was another minute that Panshin's concern grew.

He glanced right and left and started to walk away, when he heard the brisk footsteps of someone approaching. He turned, and from the distance through the mist, it was difficult to see who was coming. It could be Smithers—he was about the right size, but then again the individual coming toward him had his shoulders hunched under his trenchcoat. He was tall, as was Smithers, so it could be him. Should be him.

On the chance that it was, Panshin held his ground. Still, he felt the weight of his gun resting comfortably in his shoulder holster. His raincoat was open at the top so that he would be able to reach in quickly and draw as necessary. He was one of the fastest and most accurate shots the Soviets had. Certainly were there any danger, he would be able to react quickly enough.

The man came closer and closer, apparently paying no attention to Panshin at all. Yet Panshin felt a slow building of dread and uncertainty. He had not stayed alive, or been so effective an agent for so long, by distrusting his instincts. To play it safe he half-turned, presenting only his shoulder to the oncoming man. It was a casual enough gesture, effectively hiding that Panshin was sliding his hand towards his sleek weapon. If it was Smithers and he called out a greeting, all was well. If it was a stranger in a hurry to some other appointment, that was fine, too.

If it were anyone or anything else, Panshin was ready.

The man came closer still, and by this point Panshin knew for certain that it was not Smithers. Smithers had always had a slightly uneven stride, as if he were constantly endeavoring to glance over his shoulder without really looking. As with most traitors, he considered himself to be under constant observation. Still, paranoia was not completely unwarranted when you had the best of reasons to believe you were being watched.

The man started to walk past Panshin, but the Soviet did not relax his guard. He would wait until the man was safely past, safely out of range. Once that happened, he would then proceed on the assumption that something had happened to Smithers—

"Good assumption."

Panshin froze as a voice responded to a thought plucked from his head.

The man had stopped and was slowly turning towards Panshin.

There was a lopsided grin on his very pleasant face.

The man looked to be in his mid-thirties and had an almost avuncular air about him. His eyes were peaceful, and crinkled slightly at the edges. His face was narrow, his chin not particularly prominent. When he spoke it was with a slow, relaxed drawl that suggested the midwest.

"Sorry if I startled you, Mr. Panshin," he said apologetically. "My name's Reuel Beutel."

"Who are you?" whispered Panshin, trying not to acknowledge the surprise that this harmless looking man clearly knew who he was. His hand was now firmly on his gun but still within his coat.

"I just told y—oh, I see. You mean where did I come from, huh? Like, who am I representing, is that it?"

Panshin nodded.

"I'm with the Complex, y'see," said Beutel affably.

Panshin frowned. "No," he said, slowly shaking his head. "I know all the agents of the Complex. I don't know you."

Beutel laughed. In contrast to his pleasant demeanor, his laugh was high-pitched, nervous sounding. But he didn't look nervous. He looked in complete control, even though his hands were out, thumbs hooked into his coat pocket. If it came to a shootout, Panshin could kill Beutel before the stranger could even begin to go for his gun, wherever it might be.

"Well," and the simple word sounded three syllables long when he said it, "our little division tends to keep a low profile."

They stared at each other, Beutel's smile never wavering, his hands never moving. What did he know? Was he waiting for Panshin to crack, to spill and give something away? Obviously they did not know Panshin very well.

"What do you want?" said Panshin. His tone was

forceful, clearly indicating that he was not a man to be trifled with.

"Well," (there it was again, that teeth-gnashing drawl), "I came by to tell you that Mr. Smithers won't be coming by for, oh, the rest of his life, which ended about an hour ago." Beutel showed his teeth and made a sympathetic clucking noise with his tongue. "His storytelling to you folks got kind of uncovered, and I had to kind of kill him. Now I'm going to have to kind of kill you, which is a shame, because you seem like a nice enough fella. And I know you got a wife and four kids back in the Soviet Union, but that's the breaks."

Beutel pulled his hands from his pockets and immediately Panshin yanked his gun from concealment. It was a smooth, seamless maneuver—a second from thought to deed. It was barely enough time for him to register that Beutel's hands were still empty and then Panshin started to squeeze the trigger.

The trigger was stuck.

He was confused, but he wasn't afraid. Not yet. After all, the advantage was still his, and surely it would take but a moment to unjam the trigger.

It was then that realization dawned. The trigger was not stuck, but rather, his finger wouldn't move. He tried to squeeze the trigger and could not.

Beutel was not moving, that same, steady smile on his face. And now there was something more, a demented gleam in his eye as he watched Panshin struggle. He laughed again, that bizarre laugh of his, and then he said, "Let me help." He made a twisting motion with his hand.

Panshin's hand swung around of its own accord, the gun now aimed straight between his eyes. It was the first time, and the last, that he felt true terror.

"Now you can shoot," Beutel told him.

Panshin started to scream in protest as his finger tightened on the trigger. The blast tore off the top of his skull and he was already dead. His finger squeezed again and a second shot blew out the rest of his face.

The impact hurled him backward over the railing and he plummeted down to the highway below.

Beutel stayed right where he was and closed his eyes in pleasure as he listened to the screech of tires, the screams from underneath, the crashing of cars as one swerved out of control (because Panshin had landed on it, crashing into and splintering the windshield), another had hit the swerving one, and within seconds there was a major pileup, car after car smashing into each other, a cacophony of metal.

The air was thick with the stench of burning rubber, and with the sound of horns. Everyone was blasting their horns (two were from cars that had cracked up and the horns were simply stuck), giving mechanical voice to the frustration and anger and confusion of the drivers.

Beutel stood above it all, approaching the railing of the overpass. He looked down, taking in the sight. Then he removed a pencil from his vest pocket, tapped it against the railing. He raised his hands high above his head, brought them crashing down, and proceeded to conduct the honking as if he were performing on a concert stage.

As confusion reigned below, all was peaceful and calm and—classical—on high.

He smiled as he conducted the unaware drivers, and sighed contentedly. ''Ahhhhh . . . Mozart,'' he said.

11

"THE PROBLEM," QUINT began, "is that you're viewing your power as some sort of amorphous thing. That shouldn't be. You have to visualize it."

They were seated outside in a small field within the enclosure. And the HQ of the Complex most certainly was an enclosure. Because for all the high-tech glitz of the place, and all the apparent freedom he, along with others, was given to roam about at will, there was still a high wall that surrounded the grounds. Access was via a single main gate from the road, and there were guards there, as well as guards who wandered about the place at random times.

Quint seemed to have been taking a more and more personal interest in the progression of Chuck's training. There were the psychiatrists, of course. Then there were the psychic experts who were constantly trying to gauge the effectiveness of Chuck's abilities. Then, curiously enough, there were the men who seemed preoccupied with keeping Chuck abreast of world affairs. He found this somewhat curious, because although his nature and religion made him feel as if he should be keeping up with such things, nevertheless it seemed odd that the Complex was so concerned about it.

They knew he was a budding history teacher as well. Maybe they were doing it for that reason. Except . . . why would the Complex be training him for that?

For that matter, what the hell was the Complex training him for? He had asked that of himself time and again, and now he addressed the question to Quint.

Quint blinked. At least, Chuck thought he blinked. His eyebrows seemed to make a distinct blinking motion behind his sunglasses. "Were you listening to what I'm saying?"

"I'm concerned with what's expected of me," replied Chuck. "In this world, nothing comes free. Everything has a price tag on it. What's the price tag for all this?" He gestured around the Complex grounds.

"Why, to serve your country," said Quint evenly.

"Yeah, so you've told me. But serve has a lot of meanings. You can serve a meal, serve a tennis ball, serve notice . . . many different ways. Each with its own demands. What are the demands on me?"

Quint let out a long breath. "Chuck . . . we've had our eye on you for a while."

Chuck frowned. "How long a while?"

"Remember that ESP testing forum you participated in back at the University last year, during the summer?"

Nodding slowly, Chuck said, "Yeeeesssss. . . ."

"That was run by us."

"You?"

"Well, not me personally. A division of the Complex. Your scores came in high, Chuck. Phenomenally high. It's why I was sent to LeQuier. Unfortunate timing resulted in my getting there too late to help avert some of the . . . unpleasantness that went on."

"A delicate enough word for it," said Chuck somberly. "So I scored high. How high?"

"High enough to get our attention. High enough that we feel you can help the Complex."

"What happened to helping my country?"

Quint made a dismissive wave. "Same thing."

"And how am I expected to help?"

Quint studied him a moment. "I'll answer that if you answer a question of mine."

"You mean there's something you people don't know the answer to?" Chuck snorted in bemusement. "That certainly destroys my faith in everything. Sure—what do you want to know?"

"Why did you become a Quaker?"

Chuck stared at him. It was not the question he'd been expecting. Curiously, there was little that Quint did or said that Chuck expected. His powers gave him a knack for anticipating people and situations—but not Quint. Psychically, it was as if the man were a total zero.

"Your parents were Baptists," Quint continued, as if informing Chuck of something he didn't already know. "You converted in your teens—about the same time you took up aikido. Why? If it's not too personal."

"No, only intensely personal."

"Go ahead then."

Chuck actually found amusement in that. He pondered the answer though, trying to find a way to put it into words.

"I was conscious, even then, that there was something in me that was wrong," he said, and then quickly amended, "if not wrong, then . . . different. It was as if there was . . . I don't know . . . a constant, steady chatter somewhere in the back of my brain. I couldn't hear it, but somehow I was aware of it. Like other people's thoughts and moods, personalities and desires, all mixed up and jumbled together."

"It's part of your ability," said Quint after a moment.

"Your TK stems from it, too. It's called 'insight,' or at
least I call it that. It's being aware, or more precisely,
keyed in, to the way the world works. The world, and
everything in it. Your insight puts you at one with the
people in the world, and with the world itself. It enables
you to empathize with people, some more than others,
depending on that unpredictable thing called chemistry.
From some you receive general feelings of empathy, others you can actually discern thought impressions. By the
same token, your feelings for the world enables you to
manipulate the physical aspects of it. Your mind over matter.''

"I wish I'd known the whys and wherefores back then,"
said Chuck ruefully. "All I knew was that I felt as if I
were losing my mind. I started seeking out whatever dis-
ciplines, beliefs, schools of thought I could that I felt might
help. I experimented with a lot, including Zen Buddhism,
that kind of thing. I was unhappy, in mind and body. For
the mind, I finally decided on being a Quaker, although
to be very honest, I was never wild about that term. It's
not really an officially recognized name by the Society,
but, hell, I've gotten so used to it it doesn't matter to me
all that much anymore. I liked the feeling of community,
the message of equality among all the members of the
Society of Friends. I liked the lack of ritualistic trappings.
I liked the strong message of nonviolence because—I'm
not sure how to explain it—I had so many dark and ugly
thoughts in my mind that seemed to come from outside of
me. I needed something strong to counter that."

"And hence, the aikido," said Quint slowly.

"The aikido," nodded Chuck. "Emphasizing balance
of nature, inner spirit, and a fighting style like poetry, all
grace and artistry. The Society helped my spirit, and aikido helped both my spirit and my body. It took many, many

years of constant discipline, but I finally felt able to cope with all the . . . what did you call it . . . the empathy I felt for all those unpleasant, free-floating angers in the world. That is—''

His voice trailed off, and Quint of course knew what he was referring to. ''That is, until that night.''

Chuck turned slowly. ''My question now—what am I really being trained for?''

''To stop people like those who hurt you and Linda,'' Quint said firmly. ''To be trained for special missions that only someone of your talents could handle. You'll save the lives not only of agents who would stand much less chance of returning alive than you, but of all those who won't suffer at the hands of villains you'll be stopping. You've spoken of bearing witness, of not turning away. How can you turn away from this opportunity?''

''I'm not turning away,'' said Chuck. ''I just . . . just have to give it some thought.''

''You've had more than enough time to think about it.''

Chuck turned slowly and looked at him. ''If I were at peace with the idea,'' he said levelly, ''my TK would be functioning at my beck and call, don't you think?''

Quint had to nod.

''All right then,'' said Chuck. ''So you were saying, about envisioning something—?''

''Oh . . . right,'' said Quint, trying to get back on track. ''If you want to pick something up, don't just try to force it up. Envision a hand lifting it up. Tell your brain what you want to have happen.''

''Doesn't my brain tell me?''

''Not in this instance. Your brain is too logical, and refuses to accept the unreality of psi power, because it knows such things cannot exist. You have to inform it otherwise.''

Chuck turned and glanced at a rock. He tried to pick it up with the power of his mind, and for a moment the rock trembled and then stopped.

"You have to relax," Quint said in exasperation.

"I'm trying," moaned Chuck. "Can't you see I'm trying?"

He got to his feet and turned toward Quint, more disappointed than angry. "You'll just have to get somebody else, Mr. Quint. None of this is working." And he headed off for his quarters, Quint watching his retreating form.

"It will work," he said softly, and removed his sunglasses once he was sure no one was around. The sun, momentarily, broke through the cloud cover and shone on his colorless eyes. "I guarantee it."

12

WHEN QUINT RETURNED to his office, Reuel Beutel was there.

Quint's office was a study in simplicity. The only spark of decoration was a ship-in-a-bottle that sat on the edge of Quint's mahogany desk, a two-masted schooner that Quint had meticulously assembled when he was a kid. When he entered his office, there was Beutel, legs propped up on the edge of the desk, holding up the ship bottle and examining it.

"Put it down," said Quint in no uncertain terms.

Beutel smiled graciously and placed the bottle slowly and gently onto the desk.

Quint walked around the desk and, as he sat down, said briskly, "I assume you've attended to business."

"Of course. I always do."

"Good."

Beutel studied his fingernails for a moment. "I'm kind of curious, I must admit," he said in that pleasant, almost distant way that he had. "You know I always do the job for you."

"Yes, of course. You're one of our most valuable men, Beutel." Quint already sensed where this was going.

Beutel's hand tightened into a fist, but his voice remained level. "So what do we need him for?"

Quint sighed and leaned back in the chair. "Reuel, we've been through this already."

"Now, y'see, I know that. It's funny. I had a vague recollection that we had discussed this, yes." Beutel was chuckling to himself. "But that was several months ago, and this Simon fellow, he's just not getting the hang of it."

"He'll come around. He has potential."

"Quint," and Beutel spread his hands wide, "you've got me. When you've got butter, why settle for margarine?"

"You know why. You saw the tape, the one I ran when I first brought Simon here."

Beutel had seen it and, although he had hated to admit it, it had been pretty damned impressive. There had been Simon, seized in a rictus of fury, blowing that guy apart just by thinking it. It had been a terrifying thing to see. Terrifying not only because Simon had been capable of such an act, but because Beutel knew it was a feat that he himself could not duplicate. His psi power, while strong, was nowhere near that devastating. It had been a galling realization to make.

Quint knew it too. He knew that he had to walk a very fine line with Beutel. Beutel had been a valuable agent, as valuable as a man could be when he was a nut. Perhaps it was that same uneven mental state that was responsible for limiting Beutel's abilities.

Even limited, he had been devastating. But now Chuck Simon had come along, and the possibilities were almost beyond Quint's imaginings, and the imaginations of his superiors as well.

"The sky's the limit with Simon," said Quint, and then

softly he added, "Which shouldn't make you feel you're in an inferior position, Reuel."

"Well now, why would I think that?" asked Beutel.

"I don't know. I thought you might. I thought you might consider Simon something of a threat to your position here."

Beutel laughed, not high-pitched and nervous this time, but full and amused. "Quint, Quint, Quint," he said slowly, shaking his head as if scolding a child. "I don't know how you could possibly think that." He leaned forward, still smiling. "I'm not concerned. I'm not nervous."

The ship-in-a-bottle suddenly rose up and, before Quint could move, the bottle descended and smashed into pieces against the desk edge. Quint jumped back, throwing up his arm to shield his face from flying glass.

Beutel did not move, but instead simply sat there, that odd smile on his face. "Not nervous at all," he said. "In fact—I happen to be in a great, great mood."

He stood up and said calmly, "I'm glad we had this chat." Then he turned and walked out.

Quint let out a slow, unsteady sigh.

This was not unexpected. Beutel, never the most stable of individuals, was becoming less and less so as time passed. Simon was the way of the future and they both knew it. He had to keep Simon protected from Beutel, for Beutel represented a terrible danger to him. Although Simon's capabilities were greater, right now in a mental fight, Beutel could have him for breakfast. And he was not about to see all the time and effort he had invested in Chuck Simon go down the drain at the hands of a psychotic psi agent.

Chuck would need protection, something round the clock. But he couldn't just assign agents to him. Beutel would see that as a sign of weakness and besides, Beutel could easily take out any normal agents. Only Simon was remotely in Beutel's league, and even he wasn't really ready to take him on yet, one-on-one.

Move Simon to another facility? Possible, but again Beutel might see that as a sign of weakness, and besides, the HQ here in Virginia was the best they had. Kill Beutel? If necessary.

Quint mentally reviewed Beutel's file, recalling everything he could about him. His strengths, his weaknesses, everything. His strengths were many, his weaknesses, few. He had tested high in virtually every psi category. . . .

Except one.

Quint paused. They hadn't done much with Simon in that category either, hadn't really tested him. If Simon had a capacity for it, and Beutel did not, it might solve a lot of problems.

He picked up the phone and, when his secretary came on, he said, "Get me Jenkins in animal studies. I think I might have a use for that canine corps of his."

13

FLAMES LEAPED UP at Chuck, and screams. From the burning wreckage of Linda's house they came staggering out, their bodies charred and thick with the smell of roasted flesh. Their eye sockets were empty, their outstretched fingers missing so much skin that the bone was sticking through.

Chuck stood there, paralyzed, mouth moving but not making a sound. They advanced on him, chunks of their skin falling away revealing more of their skeletons. Their tongues were already burned away and all they could make were grisly clicking sounds with their teeth. Chuck tried to run, tried to move, but he could do nothing. He was helpless, and the closest one, with Tony's tattered and ripped clothes hanging from its body, reached out, white and jagged fingers grabbing Chuck by the throat.

Chuck sat up in bed and screamed.

He remained in that position, frozen, his heart pounding against his chest. Slowly, in the darkness of the room, his heart began to slow from its jackrabbit pace. He settled back down onto the sweat-covered sheets and waited for some sign of reaction, some commotion as a result of his cry.

There wasn't any, he realized. And there wouldn't be any. They had heard it too many times before. Too many nights had been punctuated by the howling wake-up calls of Chuck Simon. They'd gotten used to it. If anybody was staying in the other rooms nearby, they would have certainly asked to move by now. For all Chuck knew, since he rarely saw anyone, he might have the whole floor to himself.

His eyes adjusted to the darkness. But his mind had far more trouble adjusting to the reality.

They still weighed on him, after all this time. The ghosts of what had happened that awful night roamed freely through his skull, unchecked. He knew that they were the reason he was having so much difficulty consciously releasing his power. He had seen what it could lead to, was afraid that if somehow he managed to release it at will, that he would do even greater damage with it.

But on the other hand, if things continued as they had, then sooner or later the power might rise up again, in a fit of anger or fury. It had been unleashed once, and even now it could be felt bubbling below the surface, anxious to reappear. In some ways it seemed almost another part of him, almost Jekyll and Hyde-ish.

His only chance was to learn to control it at all times, in all ways. Then and only then would he be able to keep it in check.

He realized he wasn't going to be able to get any more sleep. He got out of bed and began to stretch. Then he walked, naked, over to the window and slid it open. A chill breeze wafted into the room, and he stroked at his beard which was now coming in quite nicely. It was appropriate, for these days he felt like a hermit. All he ever saw were the people who tested him, or prodded him, or probed him. He had no friends. Whenever he saw anyone else they seemed to steer clear of him, although they would toss off a friendly wave. It wasn't surprising, really. News of his abilities must have traveled quickly, and no one wanted to get too involved with someone who could collapse your body by thought alone.

But I would never do that, he told himself, and then reminded himself that he already had. And to say "I'd never do it again" didn't have quite the same impact.

He stretched his arms and legs, and felt stiffer than usual. He had been slipshod, he knew, in his maintaining of his aikido—so much else had occupied him. What he needed most was a good workout. Perhaps he could speak to Quint, have Quint provide someone to give him the kind of workout he needed.

For the moment, he could practice his kata. Kata was a series of movements that used both attacking and defending techniques. It was a way of limbering up, and restoring the naturalness of the aikido to his body.

He glanced at his clock, glowing in silent red numbers over at the other end of the room. It was 6 A.M. and soon there would be noise and activity on the grounds. There would be the support crew, the cleaning people, the secretaries, and lower level agents all moving around, hustle and bustle. And they would smile politely, perhaps greet him by name.

And there would be the silent men in the dark suits, the agents, who would also look at him and sometimes incline their heads slightly. But that was all. Unwillingly, the darkness of their beings would flow into Chuck, and it was all he could do not to be chilled to the core by them.

There was a time when Chuck would not have known why he reacted the way he did. He would have simply decided that certain people made him feel uncomfortable, and it had always seemed that he'd been a good judge of character. Now, of course, why he was such a good judge had to be totally reinterpreted.

He assumed the relaxed stance of kata, reflected briefly on the concept that everything he'd ever understood about himself was wrong, and started to go into the movements.

There were five hand and body movement sets to go through, and at first Chuck felt stiff and awkward. But slowly the old instincts began to flow into him, and from jodan he moved more smoothly into chudan, working first his upper body and hand movements and then his middle. By the time he had gone through the next two sets of movements into the diagonals of naname, he had reacquired the swiftness and certainty of his moves. He finished the routine and then started all over again, feeling he needed it.

His stomach seemed to differ. It rumbled at him in annoyance, demanding breakfast, and over in the corner next to the clock was a box of donuts that he'd been working on as he sat disconsolate and lonely the night before while watching TV.

I'm hungry, his mind said, and a chocolate donut floated towards him. He didn't even realize what was happening until he started to reach out for it, and then his conscious mind clicked in. At that moment the donut dropped to the floor.

He stood there, frozen a moment, his excitement over possibly attaining a goal momentarily overwhelming his trepidation over reaching that same goal.

So many times in recent months he had strained, given all his effort, to try and lift up or manipulate. But it should be secondary, instinctive movements, flowing just as naturally through steady repetition as his kata did.

By focusing on one, perhaps he could bring the other about more naturally.

He slid into his jodan once more, advancing his feet and swivelling his arms and body around. From jodan into chudan, and from chudan into gedan, to work the lower movements. Midway through gedan he casually framed a mental hand to pick up the donut.

Obediently the donut rose into the air, stopping at eye level. His momentary excitement caused the donut to tremble and almost fall, but then he reminded himself that this was nothing extraordinary. Not for him. An outsider might watch him run through his kata and marvel at the grace and speed of the moves, and shake their head in amazement. But for him it was second nature. Same thing now. This was nothing special. This was just something he could do. Some could paint pictures, others could discover cures for diseases, and still others could fly airplanes. That was what they could do. And he could perform aikido and float donuts. Nothing extraordinary. Take it in stride, and don't let the excitement of discovery and potential thwart you.

The donut stabilized, and Chuck decided to keep it in the air for as long as he could. From gedan he went into ushiro, and then back into naname, and slowly he devoted less and less of his efforts to keeping the donut floating until only the barest of conscious thought was required.

It reminded him of the old joke about the parachute, where one would jump with a smaller and smaller parachute until, eventually, the jumper would need no parachute at all.

He finished his kata and stood there, trying to decide what to do next. He was waiting for himself to get tired, but it wasn't happening. There was almost no physical effort at all involved in lifting the donut.

Perhaps, he realized, it was because donuts weren't especially heavy.

The donut drifted toward his mouth and he took a bite of it, then sent it gliding back to the box.

He turned toward his bed and tried to lift it. It got perhaps six inches off the ground and then Chuck gasped. Sucker was heavy.

Was it psychosomatic? Was it that, since his brain knew that he physically would have trouble lifting it, his brain was limiting itself to those same parameters? He wasn't sure. All he knew was that the bed clumped back down to the floor, uninterested in being his latest demonstration.

All right. The bed, with headboard and frame and boxspring and mattress, might be a little tough. But he had carted mattresses around enough times.

At first he started the usual process of straining but quickly stopped. To put himself back in the mood, he assumed the stance and ran through his jodan movements once more, and as he approached the end, casually envisioned hands on either side of the mattress, lifting it. The mattress obediently raised into the air.

"Turn over," he said.

The mattress swiveled in the air, the sheets falling to the boxspring.

Turn over. This time it was a purely mental command. Once again the mattress pivoted in midair.

He started to feel a physical strain, as if his own muscles were supporting it. It was a fascinating sensation. He wanted to lower the mattress back to the box spring, but then realized the sheets would be under it. While keeping the mattress levitated, he endeavored to slide the sheets out.

But he couldn't split his concentration, and the mattress *flump*ed down with a creaking of springs.

He staggered back against the cabinet and let out a long breath, and only then realized that he'd been holding his breath the entire time. That was obviously another part of doing it properly—regulating the breathing in a careful, steady manner, just as proper breathing techniques were so important in the martial arts.

Aikido came from nature, and from within. Apparently the same sort of balance, the same sort of discipline, was also going to be needed to make his TK work properly. For some reason, knowing that the two arts flowed from the same sort of base made him feel good about his mental power for the first time.

He reached down, pulled out the sheets with something as mundane as his hands, and made the bed the old-fashioned way.

He began to practice here and there, just little things. If he could control the little things, he could control the big things. When he went to the bathroom the toilet flushed itself, and the spigots turned themselves on and shut themselves off. Instead of sorting through clothes in drawers, he would lift them out and examine them in midair; at first it had been one at a time, but over a period of days it was in this manner that he learned to control more than one thing at the same time.

He tried mentally knotting a necktie, but gave up after a half-dozen failed attempts. He was miserable at handling ties in the normal way, so it made sense that he wouldn't be much better using TK.

Other little things also escaped his ability—he lacked the mental dexterity to tie his shoes (although that he could, fortunately, manage with his hands). He tried threading a needle and had problems with that. But he could lift things, put them down, have them circle the room. He had definitely made a breakthrough.

And he told no one.

Although he didn't know why, as his mind grew stronger and began to shake off the shackles of fear that he had placed on himself, certain feelings encroached more and more on him. Feelings of unease, feelings that something was wrong. That he was surrounded by great, dark fingers that were slowly coming together into a massive fist, and he would be lost, crushed into that enormous palm. Held in darkness, unable to escape.

He had taken to wearing the bent-spoon "A" on a chain around his neck, and when he went to his testings and mental workouts, he allowed some degree of his progress to show. But only a little, and even then he still made it seem far more of a strain than it was. They would tell him, as always, that he had to relax, not realizing that he had already come to that understanding. Using his TK was simply a matter of clearing his mind and letting his instincts take over and treating the ability as a matter of course rather than something freakish.

He wasn't certain just why he was holding out. But he knew that he should not tip his hand just yet.

Quint watched the videotape and nodded slowly in approval.

There was Chuck, standing several feet away from the bed and miming the gestures as the sheets neatly folded themselves into place, the pillow obediently hovering above them and waiting for the opportunity to settle back into place.

Mr. Simon had, of course, not known about the hidden camera in his room. He did not need to know that he was under twenty four-hour surveillance. Indeed, the more that Quint knew and Chuck didn't, the better he liked it.

There were also things he knew that Beutel did not know, and those were things he liked even better. Beutel was becoming a bit too sure of himself. Simon needed an ally. Beutel needed to be a little less cocksure. And Quint needed something to happen, because although things were progressing, they were not progressing quickly enough for himself or for the Council. So the timetable had to be moved forward.

He glanced at his watch, got up, and crossed to the window of his office. If everyone was on their cue, he thought, then that timetable might go a long way toward rolling forward about now.

Dr. Tyler looked up at the clock on the wall as Chuck slowly, laboriously, worked on sliding a glass across a table. At this point it was, of course, child's play for Chuck. He could have lifted a pitcher, filled the glass and drunk it, all without touching it. Again, though, he felt no reason to let Tyler or any of the others in on that.

"All right, that's enough for today," said Tyler quickly.

Chuck looked up in surprise. Not only did Tyler rarely, if ever, speak, but he never interrupted when Chuck was actually making headway with something. "I can try harder," said Chuck, starting to feel a little guilty. He was, after all, dragging things out at the doctor's expense, merely to satisfy his unexplained need for caution and secrecy.

"No. That will be all." Tyler rose, gathered up his notes, and hurriedly departed out the side door of the room.

Chuck sat there in confusion for a moment and then shrugged. Perhaps Tyler had some other appointment to attend to. No matter what it was, it certainly was not anything Chuck had to involve himself in. Lord knew he had his own problems.

He got up and went out the rear exit door.

* * *

Beutel, on orders from Quint, was standing about fifty feet away and leaning against one of the pillars of the library when Chuck emerged from the testing center. Beutel took a long drag from a filtered cigarette, then flicked on the ground and rubbed it beneath his heel.

Light a fire under him, Quint had told him. Beutel had been very pleased to hear that. He'd been concerned that Quint was treating this moron with kid gloves, and the reason for that was that this Simon guy simply didn't have what it took. Quint had obviously been unwilling to admit it, but now that he was asking for Beutel's assistance, it was clear that he was finally facing facts.

Beutel intended to do more than light a fire under him. He was going to show him who was boss around here, the head man. He was going to show Simon just why he, Beutel, was the preeminent psychic assassin of the Complex. Why he was considered the first and best weapon against such Russian agents as Genady Korsakov, the guy the Sovs had been priming for years to take a run at the American secret services.

He had come much too far to be unseated by this upstart, Simon. Beutel had been reading up on Simon's background and was appalled. A gym coach, for chrissakes? In freaking LeQuier, in the middle of nowhere Ohio? Loved, respected, a nice guy and friend to all, a peaceful Quaker who could defend himself if need be. It was enough to make Beutel's hair curl.

Beutel had not come from such a nicey-nice background. He had grown up rooting around the back alleys of the hell hole that Los Angeles had devolved into. The economic tailspin there had taken jobs, resources, even lives.

Beutel had run with one of the Wild Packs, had a rap sheet a mile long.

Eventually, as the years passed, he'd outgrown the Wild Packs, but still had buddies he hung out with. He and his pals never thought of what they did as crime. It was simply the way they survived, and they'd gotten very, very good at survival.

Then there had been that final time, a couple years ago. Him and three buddies had knocked over a convenience store, not for money—that was impossible to do these days of ID cards. They wanted something far more basic, namely the food. Cops had shown up and bullets started flying.

Something in Beutel had snapped that day. Pinned down, cornered like a rat, and he was firing back until his gun was clicking on empty.

He heard the similar unpleasant sounds from the guns of his buddies, and then five cops had come smashing in through the front window of the convenience store. Their heavy boots crunched on the glass beneath their feet, and Beutel's buddies had leaped to their feet, their hands in the air. Before they could even get out the words "We give up," the chatter of the cops' guns had split the air. His friends' bodies practically exploded under the impact of the bullets, and a shower of blood rained down on Beutel as he cowered behind the baked goods shelves.

The cops had been advancing on him then. He heard them coming as he crouched in his hiding place, and one of the cops shouted "Come out from behind there."

"They were trying to surrender, you fuck!" yelled Beutel.

"Come out from behind there," said the cop again, like a robot. And Beutel knew that he was dead now; that the moment he stuck his head out, they were going to pump it full of ammo. It wasn't like the old days that some of the men talked about, when you could get away with murder, literally, and they had to stand there and read to you some sort of shit about rights. Now they'd just as soon kill you as look at you, and they were going to look at him and kill him—

That was when the snap had occurred. He felt a surge of power start from somewhere down in the back of his brain, bubbling behind his eyes and out, roaring into the small store like a hurricane.

Stock was suddenly blasted off the shelves, flying everywhere as if they'd taken on lives of their own. Boxes of detergent, flour, powder, anything that could cause fog and confusion, leaped into the air and blew open, sending clouds of whiteness everywhere. The convenience store was filled with coughing and shouting and gagging, and no one knew where to look or what to do.

The freezer case doors leaped open and huge bags of ice ripped themselves open. Ice cubes flew out, littering the floor, and cops were going down everywhere, slipping and sliding.

Beutel started to laugh, that wild, crazy laugh that had made even fellow Wild Pack members shiver. He darted down the side aisles, all the time envisioning new and more bizarre things that could happen. Sure enough, the overhead fluorescent bulbs started to blow out, one by one. In the parking lot outside, all the car horns started to beep. Now no one could see or hear or understand what the hell was happening.

He got to within range of the front door and dashed out, cackling wildly with triumph. He glanced back as he ran, enjoying the sight of utter chaos behind him—

—and got hit by a police car that roared into the parking lot, its siren drowned out by the horns.

When he regained consciousness, he was in the hospital with compound fractures. The first thing he saw was a man in a dark suit who identified himself as being with the Complex. They had had a long and entertaining talk about what rotten condition the country was in. And then the man from the Complex told him about the reports they'd gotten of what had happened, and how they'd found it very interesting. They wanted to take him, once he'd recovered, to one of their local offices and run a battery of tests on him.

"I think my ass is probably going to jail," Beutel had told him.

The man had assured him that that was most definitely not the case. Moreover, he told Beutel, if the tests worked out, they'd want Beutel to work for them. He'd get the best clothes, and good food, free room and board, extensive travel . . .

"What do I have to do for this deal?" Beutel had asked suspiciously.

"Kill people we want you to kill," was the reply.

This, of course, was perfectly fine with Beutel.

He'd finally found something to live for, a goal to reach. And he knew why they wanted him. Because he had this crazy power, a power he wasn't going to question. Power was never to be questioned. Power was to be used. He'd never quite understood that until the night in the convenience store. It was as if he'd been reborn new and improved.

The day he checked out of the hospital he mentally pushed a janitor down a flight of stairs as he passed by. Partly he did it to see if he could, but mostly he did it for luck. The janitor's neck had snapped somewhere around the fifteenth step. Beutel smiled as all around him there was commotion, and he left quietly with the man from the

Complex who, Beutel thought, might have realized what just happened but wisely didn't say anything.

He had been with the Complex since then, working his way up. He was their premiere assassin. . . .

So what the hell did they need this Simon punk for?

He stood there, glowering at Chuck as he made his way across the grounds. This was the moment, the moment when Quint wanted him to accost Chuck and "light a fire" under him.

Light a fire, all right. He'd burn his ass off.

He started toward Chuck at a slow, easy pace, the pleasant expression he'd developed over the years now on his face. He was holding his hat in his hands, revealing the brown hair that came to a widow's peak on his forehead.

At fifteen paces away, Simon suddenly turned. He was aware. No, more than that. He was *aware*. Well, that didn't matter. Beutel mentally took measure of Simon and wasn't particularly impressed.

Sure, Beutel seemed to have reached his peak in terms of mental powers. His primary specialty was inanimate objects and wind effects. Maybe he couldn't do spectacular stuff like blow guys apart by mind power alone. But so what? Not only was stuff like that showy, but everything about Simon indicated that he didn't have the guts for the kind of life he would be asked to lead.

Beutel was certain he knew what the score was. Quint, the old dodger, was intending to use Beutel to scare Simon a few notches up the ladder. Make him feel that his life was in jeopardy and he would react accordingly.

The scenario, as Beutel saw it, could go a number of ways. No matter how it played, Quint would come out on top—

Unless Beutel could rub his nose in his failure. Sure.

Killing Simon would be too easy. But he was sure that he could terrorize Simon, have him shitting in his pants, and Simon wouldn't lift a finger to defend himself. He was afraid of the power, Simon was, and didn't trust himself to use it.

Beutel had his number easy.

Chuck saw Beutel coming and a chill ran through him. This was a man who could hurt him. A man who reeked of evil.

He slowed to a halt, rather than speed up to try to outrace him. This was not someone from whom he could run, of that he was quite sure. Besides, he had no desire to run.

Automatically his posture slid into that of preparation for potential attack. At the same time, without quite knowing how, his brain clicked into neutral. He felt the power on tap, in case he should need it.

This man had the power as well. Chuck wasn't quite sure how he knew, but he did.

"Hi," the man said, and he stopped a couple of yards away. "I don't think we've met. I'm Reuel Beutel."

"Chuck Simon."

They stood there, facing each other, hands at their sides, and Chuck got the uncanny impression that they were about to go for their guns.

"What can I do for you?" asked Chuck.

"Well," said Beutel, smiling, "you can let me kill you. Save us both a lot of time and aggravation."

From above, in his office, Quint watched it all unfold beneath him.

Now where the hell was Jenkins? Quint had emphasized to him that timing was important.

Of course, Quint's reading of Beutel's psych profile was

also important. More specifically, he was reading between
the lines. If his guess was wrong, he might be risking Simon's life. Quint didn't think Beutel would try to kill Simon,
but then again, Quint might be wrong. Beutel was bor-
derline psychotic, and if Quint had to pick a place for him,
it would be on the far side of the border. So nothing about
him was predictable, and it was entirely possible that Quint
was risking Simon at a time he couldn't afford to do so.
If Beutel cut loose, the chances were that Simon couldn't
handle him. Eventually, yes, but not at the moment.

Still, sink or swim. Sometimes you just had to take
chances.

And there, at last, was Jenkins, coming from the research center. And he had with him—

At first Quint frowned in anger. Goddamnit. Jenkins
was supposed to be working with canines. What the hell
was he doing with a horse? On a leash, yet?

Then Quint realized, and his eyes widened. "Good
Christ," he whispered.

Chuck tensed, which he knew was not the way to imple-
ment the power, but he couldn't help it. It was so insane.
Less than a year ago, the most anyone had ever threatened
him with was a punch in the nose. Now it seemed everyone and his brother was threatening to kill him. It was
starting to get on his nerves. He sought for mental balance
and was having trouble finding it. A physical threat—that
would not have intimidated him. He trusted in the reflexes
and purity of his aikido to see him through that. But here
was an individual who would attack him in another way,
a more insidious way.

With the aikido, Chuck had total control over the
strength of his defense. If he were faced with a mental

assault, with a telekinetic barrage, aikido would be useless. You can't break the wrist or shove back the arm of someone who doesn't need to lay a finger on you.

If Chuck mentally struck back at this Beutel, he might kill him. He could not, would not let that happen, ever again. He'd go mad if it did. But if he did not defend himself, Beutel could kill him.

"How do you want to die?" asked Beutel.

"Old age."

Beutel laughed oddly, a nervous, high-pitched laugh. "You are a funny guy," he drawled. "How about this. We go off, knock back some beers, then I force the beer can down your throat and explode it. Make a hell of mess, but we could get someone to clean it up. They got people on staff for that."

"I think I'll pass on that, if you don't mind."

"Oh, but I do mind," said Beutel. The air began to surge around him, as if the molecules were coming to life. "You're the new guy in town, here to show me up. Not gonna work, though."

"I'm not here to show anybody up," Chuck said, taking a step back. "Frankly, I'm not sure why I'm here."

"Why, kiddo—you're being trained to be an assassin," laughed Beutel. "Just like me. But I've been training longer and harder. And I'm going to eat you alive."

But suddenly Chuck wasn't listening. Suddenly Beutel seemed to fade into the background as something else entered the air.

It was like a beacon from a lighthouse had snapped on, bathing Chuck in its light, showing him the way.

For the briefest of moments he thought it was a trick, something that Beutel had conjured up. But no, this was pure and direct and primal. Something from the heart of nature, unsullied and unpolluted by the civilization that man had spread across the earth like an unsightly rash.

It called out to him, sounded in his head, and it was one word, a single word that carried a depth of meaning to it.

Food?

Beutel stared at Chuck as he prepared to launch a mental assault that would hurl Chuck at least a dozen feet back. The idiot was grinning. Did he realize that Beutel wasn't going to kill him, but only humiliate him?

His plan was simple. First he would toss Simon around. Then he'd mentally strip him, knot his pants around his ankles, and leave him dangling from the flagpole that stood in front of Beutel's office building. That should be enough to humiliate and terrify him for good, and if not, then Beutel could always kill him later.

Except Simon didn't seem to realize he was in danger. The idiot was smiling.

Now what was so goddamn funny?

Dr. Jenkins intensely disliked removing animals from the lab for any reason, much less prizes such as subject 666.

It had been a purely accidental designation. They had been performing experiments on animals for years, trying to find if psychic stimulation were possible on the lower orders. They had had the most success with dolphins, monkeys, and cats. Dogs were of less interest to Jenkins because they were harder to control and usually more high strung.

But there had been pressure from above to try and do more with dogs. They were more common in city settings than monkeys and, obviously, dolphins. And although cats were more responsive, it was felt that dogs had more potential for attack purposes.

Jenkins was a scholarly, retiring individual who had no idea, when he had signed on for the psychic research branch of the Complex, that he would be working with animals so steadily. Certainly he had done papers on the topic, but he hadn't intended to make it his life work. Still, it seemed important. So he worked with various chemicals, and with spinal fluid and brain fluid drawn from individuals who had appeared to test high for psychic ability. Jenkins never questioned where the samples came from, or whether the donors were voluntary, or even alive anymore. Somehow it seemed safer not to question.

Subject 665 had been a nice, pleasant manx cat who had died two days ago. Subject 666—well, the number, as some had observed, was the number of the Beast. That most certainly filled the bill of this creature, a German shepherd the size of a Pinto—the horse or the car, take your pick.

But the tests they'd run on this particular animal had been very, very promising. It had almost died after the injections, but then had slowly recovered. Not only that, but it immediately began to show responses. The maze test, for example, had been phenomenal. A slice of raw meat had been placed into a hermetically sealed box, so that no trace of the scent could be made by the dog. It had been placed at a random point in a very complex maze, and the only individual in the room had been a testing scientist who concentrated on the location of the meat, but kept hidden from view of the dog so that no visual cues could accidentally be given.

The dog had paused momentarily at the beginning of the maze, and then zeroed in on the meat as if by radar.

Scientists were suitably impressed, and other tests were

arranged. Of course, they kept the dog suitably underfed, since they wanted it to be cooperative. The downside of this was that subject 666 was frequently irritable as well, and seemed to be debating whether the scientists should be considered sources of food or possible food themselves.

When Jenkins had been ordered by Quint to bring the dog, leashed, out into the grounds at precisely 2:01 (and made damned sure to have his watch synchronized), the scientist had protested, stating that might not be a good idea. Quint's response was that it *might*, on the other hand, *be* a good idea, and Quint was in charge. Against his better judgment, Jenkins brought the animal out on schedule.

At precisely thirty seconds past 2:01, subject 666 acquired a new master.

Chuck laughed and said into the air, "Yes, I'll feed you."

Beutel turned, completely befuddled as to who in hell Chuck was talking to.

That was when there was a sound, like the roar of an airplane engine, but sharper, more staccato.

Beutel spun and then stood bolt still, terrified.

Subject 666 yanked against its leash, pulling Jenkins off his feet and to the ground. The leash slipped out of his hand and the dog pounded across the grounds, with a sound like an oncoming freight train.

Jenkins shook off the shock and looked up. There was that one agent he'd met, Bartels or something, frozen in place. There was another man there as well. Jenkins didn't pay much attention to the personnel that populated the grounds, but this man he had noticed every time he'd seen him. He wasn't like the others. All the others were grim clouds of determination. But he was a cloud of lightness, with just a surface hint of melancholy.

At the moment he was grinning and gesturing towards subject 666, and the dog was bounding towards him as if they were two long-lost brothers.

Beutel began to tremble, and he tried to fire up the psychic energy to slow the beast down. But nothing came to him, his power deserting him. He didn't know how to cope with the oncoming pile driver of animal fury. Not only that, his legs had turned to jelly, and his body had broken out into cold sweat.

He began to sneeze violently, wildly, staggering about, and then the monster left its feet. Its leap carried it the remaining distance and it smashed into Beutel. Beutel was sent hurtling back like a poker chip, rolling over a half-dozen times before skidding to a halt. He tried to get to his feet and once again the dog was on top of him, a massive paw shoving his face down into the ground.

High above, Quint actually smiled.

He had been right. Beutel was afraid of dogs.

Dogs scared him, terrified him. And Beutel, who would never be capable of admitting to such a thing, had actually manufactured a defense mechanism, namely an allergy.

It was the most wonderful thing that Quint had ever seen. The Complex's top assassin, screaming in terror because of a dog. Granted a big dog, a dog that might give a platoon of Marines hesitation, but a dog nevertheless. Beutel could not even begin to muster a defense, so mentally paralyzed was he by his phobia. As to its origins, Quint could not care less. Perhaps he had been left alone in a stroller when he was infant and a dog had terrorized him. Maybe his family had been eaten by dogs, for pity's sake. Who cared? It was there and it was wonderful, because Quint could make use of it.

It was a glorious moment. When Beutel slithered back to Quint's office, Quint would use that undoubtedly low moment of Beutel's life to really stick it to him. To remind him who was in charge, and who should be making an effort to stay in line. And by the way, Quint would inform him, it's obvious that you should stay the hell away from Simon.

It was such a joyous occasion that it took him a few moments to realize Beutel was about to be killed.

Beutel heard a great deal of screaming, and it took a few moments for him to realize that it was himself.

It was the barking more than anything that really got to him, a sound that filled him with dread, that scrambled his brain and simply short-circuited him. The animal's saliva dripped onto his face as the creature thrust its maw toward him and barked again and again. Then it growled like a diesel engine and bared its teeth.

Oh God I'm gonna die I'm gonna die I'm gonna die thought Beutel, frozen beyond capacity for any thought other than that.

Chuck realized he only had a second to react—

—and in that second, saw the possibility of ridding himself very quickly and efficiently of someone who could prove a danger to him. Who, indeed, had been threatening his life.

And it would not be his fault. The dog did it. All he had to do was stand back—

—and watch. And witness.

Damn, he thought, and because he was so upset, *Goddamn*, and he shouted "NO!"

The dog froze, its mouth poised over the ashen face of Beutel.

NO?

The question sounded inside his head.

It was not so much that Chuck was hearing specific words, at least not yet. It was as if his mind was interpreting for him the general thoughts, wants, desires of the animal.

The dog tilted its huge head, and Chuck noted with silent amusement the "z" shape that colored the fur on it.

No? the dog asked again. The link between them was tenuous but sure, like the first strands of a spider's web. Chuck could already feel them growing in strength and durability with every passing moment.

From beneath the animal the petrified Beutel was whimpering, and in a hoarse whisper he was saying "Please . . . please, get it off me."

Chuck sensed waves of fear pouring from Beutel, so thick and overpowering that it was all Chuck could do not to let it influence him. But he felt no fear of the animal.

"No," Chuck said firmly.

Beutel gurgled in terror, thinking that Chuck had addressed his question. But both Chuck and the animal knew what had been said. The bond was growing faster and faster, invisible tendrils forming between them.

Chuck felt the primal energy of the dog in his mind, a force of nature barely contained in a body designed for raw power. The animal was searching for ways to express itself, to communicate more efficiently. Form and concepts, ideas with no words, bubbled up in Chuck's consciousness as the dog's mind wandered through it eagerly, anxious and hungry for the new experience. Chuck's instinctive reaction was to try and block it off, as if the link were some sort of violation. But he brushed aside that gut instinct and lowered his automatic defenses. As if removed from a leash the dog began to romp through Chuck's mind, probing and pushing, excited as a kid in a candy store. There was no threat to it, but rather almost an innocence. Chuck smiled inwardly in amusement.

He reached out mentally to the dog, entering the animal's mind. It was, of course, far less complex, all instinct and raw energy.

And Chuck's mind immediately recoiled. There was the killer instinct, naked and throbbing right on the surface. And the other primal urges.

Man spent countless years discussing subtleties of philosophy and what man's yearnings and desires were. For the dog, it was far simpler. If the dog encountered something, anything, it immediately ran the new something through a rigorous mental questionnaire, which ran roughly along these lines:

1) Should it be eaten?

2) Should it be killed?

3) Should it be killed and eaten?

4) Should it be defecated on?

5) Should it be humped?

That was it. Chuck found almost nothing in the dog's imperatives beyond that, and usually if the answer to all of the preceeding was "No," the dog would show no interest in it. Immediately Chuck wondered—not without justifiable nervousness—which one he fell into. Then he realized that there was a subtle permutation to the first consideration which was, namely: Could this provide something to be eaten? And that was where he fit in. Which, considering the alternatives, was something of a relief.

But there had to be more to existence than that, and in the mere seconds in which all of their communication occurred, Chuck tried to infuse something of himself, tried to provide some measure of man's perspective in the great realm of creation.

In a way, the two-way communication between Chuck Simon and subject 666 was the purest, most historic communion between man and animal since a hungry wolf had first wandered out of the forest primeval to seek the warmth of a fire and, in so doing, volunteered its service to the primitive man glowering on the other side of the flame.

The dog, for its part in this momentous exchange, seemed less than impressed. Chuck, on the other hand, suddenly felt the urge to scratch under his collar. Could be worse, he reasoned. At least he wasn't feeling compelled to lick his genitals.

The dog was becoming impatient and, to Chuck's surprise, more comprehensible sentences began to form in his head. The dog, of course, did not question as it thought, *Kill this one. Wants to hurt the us.*

"No," said Chuck again, as firmly as he could. "No killing. Leave him be."

The dog growled, clearly not liking the decision.

And then, the dog thought, *Look over there.*

Chuck almost looked and then stopped himself as a shriek from Beutel alerted him. The moment Chuck had started to turn away, the dog had clamped its jaws down on Beutel's throat. But as Chuck turned back the dog stopped, frozen guiltily, as if caught in the act of something as mundane as taking a dump on the living room couch.

"You tried to trick me," said Chuck incredulously.
"You son of a bitch." Which, he promptly realized, was
a pretty pointless epithet to use on a dog. Then, as sternly
as he could, he said, "Let him go. Back off, dammit. I
mean it. Back off him."

The dog was fighting it, with every part of its being. It
wanted to kill, desperately. It sensed the urgency of the
threat that Beutel posed and its every instinct was to eliminate the threat by the most expeditious means possible.

But Chuck had infused something of himself into the
animal's mind, and as long as Chuck was there, as long
as Chuck was concentrating and in the dog's presence, he
couldn't overwhelm Chuck's control. It was a major strain
for Chuck, and it opened up mental resources within him
he didn't even know he had. It was the most arduous direct
broadcasting he had ever done, and in the future such psychic workouts would serve him in good stead. For now,
all he cared about was having no more blood on his hands.

"This is your last warning," said Chuck. "Back off, or
no food."

That sucks, the dog thought dimly.

Chuck fought off amusement. Had the dog really thought
that, or did Chuck's mind simply interpret it that way?
Either way it couldn't distract him. "I know it sucks. Now
do it."

Beutel was looking from man to dog and back in total
confusion, not sure what in hell was happening. All he
knew was that one moment the dog was atop him, the next
the dog had moved off. It stopped several feet away, still
within easy striking distance, growling warningly.

Beutel knew, without fully understanding how he knew,
that the dog had keyed in on him somehow. It was as if
the dog had picked up a psychic scent. If Beutel tried

anything, the dog would react immediately. The very thought of that monster coming at him was paralyzing in and of itself.

It had been Beutel's secret embarrassment, this phobia of dogs. He had successfully covered it for years. Now it stood revealed, for all to see.

Slowly he got to his feet, still trembling as he never took his eyes from the animal's steady glare. Chuck stepped over next to the dog, giving out a silent message— screw with me, you screw with my monster here.

Beutel spread wide his hands, a lopsided grin on his face. "Hey . . . just kidding," he said. "Can't you guys take a joke?"

Neither animal nor master made any reply, and Beutel turned and walked away across the grounds.

They watched him go and then the dog looked up at Chuck. *Where's the food?*

"Come on," said Chuck tightly. "We're going to get some right now."

Quint saw them coming and, seeing the two of them together, he began to wonder if he hadn't made an error in judgement. No, definitely not, he decided—seeing Beutel humiliated like that made it all worthwhile.

He sat behind his desk, fingers steepled, and eventually he heard urgent shouts from his male secretary outside. Shouts followed by loud barks that effectively silenced them.

The doors blew open and Chuck walked in, the dog at his side. They stood there, Chuck with his arms folded, the dog eerily silent now.

* * *

The dog looked up at Chuck. *I smell him, but I don't see him*, said the dog.

Chuck looked at the dog in confusion. "What do you mean you don't see him?"

"What your four-legged friend means, Mr. Simon," said Quint, immediately perceiving to whom Chuck was talking, "is that I give out no aura."

"What?"

Slowly, Quint stood. "Virtually all humans project auras," he said in that odd, whispery voice he had. "Psychically gifted humans project stronger auras than most, which is how psychics can generally detect each other's presence, even if they don't see each other. I, on the other hand, project nothing. Call it a reverse of the ability you have."

"That's why I can never get a feeling of what you're thinking," said Chuck.

"Yes. It's also why I can generally come and go as I please. I blend in extremely well. You instinctively realized it, but you let that realization become cluttered with the mundane concerns of humanity. The animal there doesn't let himself become distracted with such trivialities."

"He's hungry," said Chuck tonelessly.

Without a word, Quint reached into his desk drawer and pulled out a pair of large, raw steaks. He tossed them to the floor in front of the dog, who greedily began to consume them.

"You're prepared for anything, aren't you?" said Chuck.

"Yes."

"You prepared to answer questions? Like whether what Beutel said was accurate. Am I really being trained to be an assassin?"

Quint did not answer immediately. Instead he held up a newspaper that had been sitting on his desk and tapped the headline. "Have you heard about this man?"

Chuck, not understanding, nevertheless looked at the paper. Pictured just below the headline was a black and white photo of a particularly notorious dictator of a South American country. The headline screamed of some recent atrocities performed in his name.

Chuck stared at the newspaper. The dog, for his part, since he could not eat, kill, or hump the newspaper, and at the moment had no need to defecate, paid no attention at all. He had already consumed the first steak and was greedily at work on the second.

"What about him?" asked Chuck.

"He's going to be coming to D.C.," said Quint. "Our noble leaders are actually considering trying to reason with this madman. For us, of course, it is a golden opportunity." He tapped the newspaper. "Thousands dead, Chuck. Thousands at his hands. You can do something about it."

"No," said Chuck.

"All you would have to do is stop his heart. He keels over, dead. All the autopsies in the world would not indicate anything other than that."

"No," said Chuck again.

"Dammit, man," said Quint with a flare of anger, which was met with a low growl from the dog. Quint promptly lowered his voice, and continued, "Didn't you hear what I said? This man has no regard for human life. When you witness something, you're supposed to do something about it. The world is witnessing this man's atrocities, and no one is doing anything about it. You can."

"An eye for an eye, is that it?" asked Chuck coldly.

"Straight from the Bible," said Quint.

"You a religious man, Quint?"

"When I have to be."

"Good. Then when I tell you to go to hell, you'll understand the full implications."

Slowly Quint removed his sunglasses, and Chuck trembled slightly as he saw the colorless tone of Quint's eyes. But he stood his ground and said, "You lied to me, Quint. You knew I wouldn't cooperate with something like this and you lied to me."

"And you haven't been less than honest with me?" retorted Quint. "You established psychic rapport with the dog quickly enough. The doors to my office flew open at your command. You've been holding out on us, Chuck. And look at all that I've done for you. When you came here, you were a mental wreck. We sorted things out for you, trained you, and guided you. When Beutel threatened you, I arranged for you to acquire your partner there. Unless you thought that happened by coincidence. Nothing happens around here unless I want it to, Chuck."

Chuck looked down at the dog, who had finished its meal (not its meal, *his* meal, Chuck realized) and was now staring up at Chuck with a look of open curiosity. Chuck almost felt as if, given the circumstances, he should tell Quint to take the dog and—

You wouldn't.

The dog actually looked hurt and Chuck smiled slightly. "Of course not." Then he turned back and glowered at Quint. "But I won't do what you want, either. I'll never kill anyone with my power again."

"Even if, by so doing, you could save thousands, perhaps millions of others."

Slowly Chuck nodded.

In contrast, Quint shook his head. "I expected better of you, Chuck."

"Sorry to disappoint you."

"No, it's all right," said Quint. "We'll just have to find something else for you to do."

Chuck's eyes narrowed. "What do you mean, something else?"

"It should be obvious. We originally thought of you as a potential assassin. If that won't work out, then we can find something else for you. Surveillance, for example. Or perhaps search-and-seizure squads—you'd be excellent for something like that."

Chuck was uncertain. He couldn't shake the feeling that Quint was lying, but, unable to detect any readings from him one way or the other, he couldn't be certain.

"I'll think about it," said Chuck slowly, "but we've got to get something straight. It has to be total honesty between us, from here on out. If there's anything you haven't told me, now is the time to say it."

Quint replaced his sunglasses and Chuck breathed an inward sigh of relief.

"There's nothing else," said Quint. "Trust me."

14

When Agent Jeffries stepped off the train, Reuel Beutel was there to meet him.

Jeffries blinked in surprise. He had seen Beutel around every now and then, during the brief times when Jeffries was not out in the field. But he'd always gotten the impression that Beutel was a heavy player, someone who was only called in when there was some serious shit going down. So why would Beutel be acting as a messenger boy, doing something as mundane as picking Jeffries up at the station?

Beutel extended a hand and pumped Jeffries'. "Good to see you, Jeffries," he said formally. "We've heard a great many good things about you. Welcome to Virginia."

"I've been here before," said Jeffries bemusedly, "although not for a long while. In fact, I was somewhat surprised Quint called me in."

"Why?"

"Well, because I'd spent a month getting in deep with the terrorist gang in Denver. I was that close to finding out who their backing was. Then to have it yanked out from under me . . ."

Beutel shrugged expansively, and then grinned. "I guess

you might say it's all too complex for me. Get it? Complex?'' He elbowed Jeffries in the ribs and chuckled at his not-particularly-funny joke. Jeffries merely grimaced and held his traveling bag tighter on his shoulder.

Quint's message had been very specific. Come to Virginia on a very specific train. Make no attempt to verbally confirm, as there was a serious security leak. Jeffries would have doubted the veracity of it all, had the message also not featured certain key code words that confirmed the seriousness of the situation.

They made their way out to the parking lot and to Beutel's sporty runabout. Beutel popped the trunk and Jeffries tossed in his carrying bag.

''So, what's the story?'' asked Jeffries as Beutel expertly backed the car out.

''Afraid I couldn't tell you, chief. Everything is on a need-to-know basis. You're going to have to wait until we get to HQ to be debriefed.''

Jeffries nodded. That sounded like standard operating procedure, right enough. He settled back in the comfortable seat and folded his arms.

Beutel seemed interested in making casual small talk, and Jeffries did the best he could to respond. His mind, though, was not particularly on the subject of conversation. Instead he was busy regretting his abortive assignment.

Lately it seemed all he had was regrets. Regrets over what had happened to Tony back in Ohio. Regrets over this unfinished job. Regrets over his entire career path. He was beginning to wonder if he hadn't made a major mistake, and if perhaps there wasn't some way to get out of all this.

Resign? Was that possible? He'd heard of people who had resigned. He'd also heard of people who wanted to resign but were simply reassigned—and just what was that a euphemism for?

Before he knew it, the car was swinging in through the front gates of HQ. Beutel flashed his identification and the guards waved them through.

At a place where the driveway curved in two different directions, Beutel took the left curve. This surprised Jeffries, who sat up in confusion and said, "Wait . . . isn't Quint in Bravo Building? Shouldn't we be heading to the right?"

"Special procedures," said Beutel.

Jeffries shrugged. That was certainly nothing new with this outfit. The least little thing prompted all types of different procedures, as if to throw a great, unseen enemy off the track. Sometimes, Jeffries thought, they did it all just to show how secret and clever they could be. Entire thing was a colossal waste of time, if you asked him.

Beutel swung them around into the parking field behind the residence hall and then killed the engine. He sat there a moment, flexing his fingers on the steering wheel, and Jeffries looked at him curiously. "You okay?"

"Fine," said Beutel, turning and smiling, an innocuous expression on his face. "Just thinking of everything that has to be done. Lot of business to attend to."

They sat there a moment or two longer as a roving MP rolled past on a motorcycle. It was such a curious combination, with the highly conspicuous uniformed military men stationed on grounds that were replete with agents proficient in subterfuge. It was like cruising a city in an unmarked car that had the words I'M A SPY stenciled across the hood. Still, the Complex generally didn't worry about such petty concerns.

The moment the MP had passed, Beutel got out of the car. Jeffries followed him and Beutel trotted briskly toward the large residence building. Jeffries wanted to know what the hell was going on but Beutel gestured quickly that Jeffries should be right behind. Confused but willing, Jeffries entered the tall, ten-story building through the door that Beutel was holding open for him. Beutel went in after him.

As they stepped into the elevator, Jeffries said, "So what's the story here?"

"Quint is having his office swept for bugs," replied Beutel, watching as the indicator lights flashed. The elevator car bore them up towards the tenth floor.

"He thinks his office is bugged?" said Jeffries incredulously. "How? Security in that building is tight as a drum."

"Doesn't know how, but you don't question Quint," said Beutel with a shrug. "He temporarily relocated over here."

"I think he's losing it," said Jeffries, shaking his head. "I mean it. The guy's always given me the creeps in the first place, but I think he's really going over the edge at this point."

Beutel slowly nodded. "I really hate to admit it," he said thoughtfully, "because he's such a fine agent and supervisor—but you might be right. The strain of everything he's up to—frankly, I'm not entirely surprised. But we can discuss that later. For now, I know he's really anxious to talk to you."

"About what?"

Beutel laughed. "Y'got me."

They got out of the elevator and started down the corridor. As they got to the Emergency Exit stairwell, Beutel suddenly snapped his finger. "Now isn't that the luck," he said in irritation.

Jeffries looked at him, puzzled. "What's wrong?"

"There's something I forgot to do. Just remembered. It's on the floor right below this one, I'll be right back. Tell ya what—he's right up there," and he pointed to a room. "Go up and knock, he's expecting you. Tell him I'll be up in five minutes."

"I could just wait for you—" Jeffries began.

"Nah, you just go on ahead. Shouldn't hold up the show any longer than necessary. Y'know how he gets."

"Sure do," nodded Jeffries, and headed for the door as Beutel stepped into the stairwell, letting the door swing shut behind himself.

Jeffries knocked on the door, setting into motion the events that would lead to his death within the next five minutes.

15

"YOU NEED A name."

The dog looked up. His muzzle had been resting on his paws as he watched a rerun of "Lassie." Chuck was lying back in his bed, mentally threading a needle, removing the thread and then doing it again.

He was extremely pleased that his mental dexterity had grown. He attributed it entirely to his constant exposure to the dog. The mental stimulation of communicating on an ongoing basis with the animal had been a steady workout such as he had never gotten. At the end of the first day he had gone to bed with a pounding headache, but by this point, close to two weeks later, it was as natural as breathing.

The mind, like the body, benefited from constant exercise. Communication with the dog had not only improved his TK skills, but his mind sensitivity had grown. His perceptions and interpretations of thoughts were even sharper than before. His powers had always given him that low level "buzz," the background noise that had pushed him to discover ways such as Quakerism and aikido to cope. For he did not have the mental dexterity to distance himself from it, sort through it, and deal with it. Now, though, he did. He was like a radio that was missing its tuner, and the dog had provided the missing part. By the same token, the dog's communication abilities had grown tremendously. Either that, or Chuck's skills at interpreting his broadcasts had improved; it was difficult to say.

The dog, he realized as he thought about it. All this time, and the dog and he had simply *thought* at each other. Oh, Chuck still spoke out loud to aid himself, the same as many deaf sign translators who say what they are signing to help keep their thoughts orderly. But the real communication was mind-to-mind, so he had never had the occasion, or need, to address the dog by a name.

Besides, saying "Come here fill-in-the-blank" was unnecessary, since he and the dog had been inseparable since they'd first met. It had royally pissed off Jenkins, but those were the breaks. Quint had been firm with Jenkins and that was, quite simply, that.

Still, inseparable or not, Chuck began to feel he'd been remiss. "You need a name," he said again.

A what?

"A name. Something I can call you."

Why?

"So we can communicate."

We communicate now. What's a name?

"You know perfectly well. It's something that humans use to identify themselves, something they call each other so they know who they're talking to."

Are you talking to any other dogs?

"No," laughed Chuck.

Well, I'm not talking to any other humans. I don't need a name.

"It's traditional."

Is talking to a dog traditional?

"No. Well, yes, but having the dog talk back isn't."

The dog stared at him a long moment. *When is lunch?*

"I'm not dropping this. I'm giving you a name."

Can I have lunch afterward?

"You already had lunch."

Not recently.

Chuck sighed and stroked his chin, noting once again the "Z" shape on the dog's forehead. He could call the animal "Zorro," he supposed, but somehow it didn't seem right. Zorro was the fox; wily, cunning and sleek, elusive and tricky. The dog was none of those things. He was much more like a Sherman tank than a fox. Call him Sherman? God, no . . .

A fox and a tank? Why did that ring a bell?

He clapped his hands together happily. "Rommel!" he said.

The dog cocked his head. *What?*

"Rommel," he said. "A famous tank commander in World War II. General Rommel, and he was called the Desert Fox. And he was a German, and you're German— well, a German shepherd, at any rate. How does Rommel sound?"

Who cares?

"It's important to me," said Chuck.

The dog sighed, making a soft whine in his throat. *If I like it, can I eat?*

"Yes."

I love it. Where's lunch?

Chuck laughed. "Don't you want to call me something?"

No.

"You can call me Chuck."

I'd rather be neutered.

Chuck was surprised. "You know about animals being neutered?"

I've been around. Met a few.

"You could tell?"

Rommel gave him a look that dripped disdain. *You're kidding, right? That can't be missed.*

Then Rommel glanced up at him with a look that, even if Chuck hadn't been able to exchange thoughts, would have been clear. "I wouldn't try to have that done to you," said Chuck quickly. "I mean, you wouldn't want that, right?"

Only if you tried it out first.

At that moment there was a knock at the door, two quick efficient raps. Chuck glanced at the door and then looked at Rommel. "You expecting company?"

I'm expecting lunch.

"God, a one-track mind."

As he spoke he crossed to the door and opened it.

For a fraction of an instant, he did not recognize the man at the door, nor did the newcomer know Chuck.

Then the man gasped and cried out, "You!" As he did so, he had yanked a gun from his shoulder holster and was bringing it around to bear on Chuck.

Jeffries could not believe it.

The door had been opened by the psychic killer, the man whose image had haunted many of his waking and sleeping hours since the hideous events in LeQuier.

Jeffries had known all along that Simon had been set up, that it had all been arranged so that he could be drafted into the Complex. That had been the riff going in. The problem was that he had dwelled on it so long, built up such a terror of the man in his mind during the time, that his actions were automatic, done without thinking.

He went for his gun, yanking it from his shoulder holster and brought it around to aim at Chuck. It was a stupid move, he would realize during the remaining four minutes, thirty seconds of his life, but at this point it was the move that came to him naturally.

Just as Jeffries brought the gun around, an invisible force grabbed him by the arm, swinging the gun wide of his target. From behind Simon, Jeffries heard barking so loud it suggested a dog of mammoth proportions, and it did not sound happy. That, combined with Simon's calm gaze and his own terror at losing control over his weapon, caused his trigger finger to squeeze spasmodically. The gun went off, blasting apart a rather tacky painting that was hung (bolted, actually) on the wall.

"Drop it," said Simon calmly.

Jeffries' fingers were pried apart, and the gun fell to the floor.

Simon didn't even let him get near, instead embracing his entire body in a vise-like grip conjured from his mind. Jeffries gasped and struggled—

And Chuck gasped as well.

Chuck's sudden mental distress, combined with the overt attack of the gun-wielding human, was more than enough to propel Rommel forward, but Chuck's body was in between him and the attacker.

Out of my way, Rommel growled.

"No," snapped Chuck. "Rommel, stay where you are."

The terror of the man's thoughts had invaded Chuck's mind. Terror, and free-floating anxiety, images, so many concerning Chuck that it was easy for him to discern them.

Chuck had not recognized the man at first. After all, he'd never had a chance to see him clearly back in Le-Quier. But here the random franticness of his thoughts were clear to Chuck. The chaotic nature of fear, Chuck would realize later, usually made it easier for Chuck to skim specifics off the top, since there was so much activity and so little control.

What he was skimming now was pure scum.

"You were there," Chuck said tightly.

"No . . ." Jeffries began.

Suddenly Jeffries was propelled upward, slamming against the ceiling. He cried out.

Give him to me, Rommel urged.

Chuck ignored him, for his attention was partially distracted. Behind the painting that had been shot apart, inset into the wall, were the sparking remains of what appeared to be some sort of video camera set up.

"Those bastards," muttered Chuck.

And Rommel keyed off of Chuck's anger. *I'll kill them all.*

"No!" Chuck said abruptly. "No, Rommel."

He looked up at the man spread-eagled on the ceiling. "But you would know all about killing, wouldn't you?" he said tightly. "What are you doing here?"

Jeffries whimpered, certain he was going to be blown apart at any moment, like an overinflated tire.

From his jacket pocket, his ID fell out. Chuck kept him up there while telekinetically snagging the ID. In more leisurely moments, he might have been proud of how much he had improved in such a short time. Now, though, his sole concern was with the man plastered against his ceiling.

He opened the ID, already half-suspecting what he would find. He was right.

"You're an agent," he whispered.

"That's . . . that's right," and Jeffries tried to recoup some of his bravado. "So you better put me down right now—"

"Shut up," snapped Chuck, his mind racing, discerning bits and pieces of the truth from Jeffries' scrambled thoughts. The conclusion he had come to was a truly horrifying one, and it took him a moment to actually be able to voice it. "The other man—all of them—they were agents too, weren't they?"

Jeffries said nothing. Chuck lowered him slightly, then slammed him harder against the ceiling and Jeffries cried out, "Yes!"

"It was all a set-up." He couldn't believe it. "You picked one of my best athletes, knowing that that would be sure to get me involved, and got him tanked out. And the police—you people went to the cops and had them steer clear of it all. You wanted me all the time."

"Psychic powers only manifest in the right kind of situations," grunted Jeffries. "Heavy stress. Real danger. It's—unnhhh!"

Chuck was pressing him more tightly against the ceiling as he pulled on his shoes. "That's it. I'm getting out of this place. Come on, Rommel. We're resigning."

"They . . . won't let you. . . ."

"I'm not asking their permission."

He stormed out the door, Rommel right behind him.

Down in the stairwell, Beutel was hiding.

He was a full floor down, and fighting to clear his mind of any aggressive or angry thoughts. Or any thoughts at all. He wanted to do nothing to attract the attention of Simon or, even worse, Simon's dog.

He heard the gun shot, door slam, words exchanged, and then someone stormed down the hallway, past the door. Beutel staggered slightly under the overwhelming wave of psychic fury that was pouring out of Simon and the four-footed monster. Then it was gone as Simon went to the elevator, got inside, and started heading down.

Beutel smiled as he ran up the stairs. Obviously he needn't have worried. Simon had been so angry, so wrapped up in fury of his discoveries, that he hadn't noticed Beutel's presence at all.

Which was just fine.

Jeffries lay gasping on the floor and then looked up in confusion when Beutel walked in, smiling. Calmly, Beutel closed the door behind them.

"What the fuck is going on?!" shouted Jeffries. "What's happening?!"

"Weeelllll, I'm afraid I wasn't totally straight with you," said Beutel, looking embarrassed. "Quint is so big on setting people up, maneuvering things. I didn't realize until later that he set up the whole business with me 'lighting a fire,' just so I could go head to head with that goddamn dog. So I felt it was payback time. That's why I summoned you. It was all a set-up."

"I'll pay you back, you fucker!" and Jeffries lunged toward Beutel.

Suddenly Jeffries' necktie tightened around his neck. Jeffries gasped, clawing at it, uncomprehending, and then the ends of the tie, the aprons, went straight up into the air.

Jeffries was yanked completely off his feet, kicking and grasping. The necktie swung around behind him and he couldn't get at it, and now he couldn't get air into his lungs either.

He choked and gagged, his eyes bulging out in terror. He kicked in futility, hands lashing out, but there was nothing to grab. His neck closed in on him, throat being crushed as his weight dragged him down against the stranglehold of his tie. The world hazed out around him.

"Aren't necktie parties fun?" said Beutel conversationally.

He watched Jeffries dance on air for a brief time, because there wasn't all that much time to waste. The moment he was sure Jeffries was dead, or near enough to dead so that Beutel was comfortable, he mentally gripped Jeffries by the seat of his pants, while still keeping a grip on the necktie.

He made a quick pass with his right hand, and the body sailed toward the full length window at top speed.

Jeffries' body slammed against it and smashed through. Beutel released his grip and the corpse sailed out and down, plummeting toward the square far below to land with a sickening thud.

Beutel smiled. Already from far below he could hear shouting, the sound of running feet, confusion and yelling. Barked orders as all the little mundanes scrambled around trying to determine what's what.

"Quint," he said, smiling, "two can play at this game."

16

CHUCK STORMED OUT of the building and stopped dead.

Things on the grounds were usually so low key, so laid back and secretive, that the place gave the illusion of almost being deserted. Now, though, that was clearly not the case. The main square was mobbed with scientists, with men in dark suits, but mostly with MPs. The soldiers clustered around, lots of them, their weapons no longer slung but instead gripped tightly, looking around for trouble.

A number of them were looking up, and automatically Chuck did as well. He saw the residence hall, a tower of glass like most of the other buildings on the grounds. But there was a puncture in the tower now, a hole. Someone had shattered one of the windows, about midway along the tenth floor.

"Looks like your room, doesn't it, Chuck?"

It was Quint, standing right at his elbow. Chuck stepped back, Rommel growling behind him, "Yeah, maybe. But that's not the—"

"Care to explain this?" asked Quint, not showing the least interest in what Chuck had to say. He called out to the soldiers to back away from the area they were clustered around, and they did so.

Chuck stared, shocked, at the body that lay shattered on the ground. "How did he get down there?" he demanded.

"You recognize him?" asked Quint, who still hadn't figured out just why the hell Jeffries had come in.

"You know I do!" said Chuck hotly. "You know he's one of the men who set the whole thing up. You and your whole rotten little plan. This is one of those times, Quint, when you should drop to your knees and thank God that I really, truly do hate violence. Or I would send you straight to hell, and that would only be doing God's work because that's where he's going to send you anyway."

He spun on his heel and started to walk away, fists clenched, trying to calm himself down as he did so. Rommel was right on his heels.

From behind him came Quint's soft voice, carrying in the sudden stillness of the air. "Where are you going, Chuck?"

"I quit! I resign! I've had it with this whole scummy business!" he shouted over his shoulder. "I feel dirty every time I think of my association with you people."

The abrupt, almost unanimous sound of multiple rounds of ammo being chambered brought him to a halt.

He turned slowly, and every MP, and there had to be at least three dozen of them, had their rifles aimed at him. A number of men in dark suits also had handguns out and pointed.

Quint, by contrast, stood in leisurely calm, his hands in his pockets.

"I'm afraid you are not allowed to do that."

It was all Chuck could do to mentally restrain Rommel. The dog wanted to leap directly into the jaws of the threat.

Chuck knew that those jaws would chew up the animal and spit him back out.

And there were too many guns, good God, far too many. Even though he could now handle multiple objects, there was no way in hell that Chuck was going to be able to stop all of the attackers.

"This is America," said Chuck tightly. "I can do what I want."

At that, Quint laughed. "Chuck," he said, "you're young. You don't fully understand the way things are, as opposed to the way they used to be. Hell, people weren't allowed to do what they wanted even back in the days when they *were* allowed to do what they wanted. Understand?"

"What I understand is that you are not to be trusted," said Chuck. "You've been maneuvering me and using me from the get-go."

"And now you're going to get-gone, is that is?" Behind his sunglasses, Quint frowned. "Who do you think you are? Some sort of comic book hero? Once you were humble Chuck Simon, but now you're—" And he dropped his voice to a booming bass, "Psi-Man! Able to leap towering dilemmas in a single bound! And we'll paint a large red 'P' on your chest."

Rommel took a step toward Quint, and Chuck placed a hand on the back of Rommel's neck, stopping him. Rommel growled.

"Listen, Psi-Man," said Quint, startlingly calm. "Let's fill you in on things. First, you have a power. Second, you can use it to dispose of enemies of the United States of America. If you loved your country, you would understand that. Third, you whine and preach about non-violence, but you don't seem to have any trouble with it when it's something you want—such as hurling our men out of windows.''

"I didn't do it," said Chuck tightly.

"No, he jumped. All right, Psi-Man." The name was drenched in sarcasm. "Bottom line—you're not going anywhere. I've invested a lot of time and energy in you because of what you can do, but don't misinterpret that attention. I am more than willing to cut bait if I have to. Now—are you going to cooperate?''

"No," was the terse reply.

Quint sighed. He hated to admit failure, hated to admit when things weren't working out. But this was clearly one of those times. Still, he could give it one last try.

"Chuck," he said, "I think I can still salvage this. You don't want to think about moral dilemmas, and I don't want you to have to. We have new procedures we're developing—we can deaden parts of your brain so you won't be bothered by certain ethical considerations.''

His voice a harsh whisper, Chuck said, "You're talking about a lobotomy."

"It would be tricky," admitted Quint. "After all, we wouldn't want to chance damaging your psi ability. But on the other hand, if I order these men to open fire, they're going to be performing a major lobotomy all over your body. Your choice, Psi-Man . . . unless you think bullets will bounce off your indestructable form.''

Chuck looked around desperately. The gun barrels were unwavering, the soldiers unblinking. Quint was the picture of calm, and why not? All he had to lose was some time invested. For him it would simply be a project that hadn't worked out.

We've got to kill them, said Rommel.

"No killing," whispered Chuck. "Even if I die, no killing.''

If you die, I don't get fed.

"Thanks for keeping things in perspective."

For a few brief moments, as if giving Chuck a final glimpse of something beautiful, the clouds broke. Sunbeams streamed through, one of the rare instances where they managed to overcome the haze and pollution. The sun glinted off the highly polished buildings, bathing them in a corona of light.

"Chuck," Quint said softly, "time's up."

17

BEUTEL, FEELING THAT keeping a low profile was the best procedure, was sitting contentedly in the stairwell, waiting for the sounds of rifle fire that would spell the end of Chuck Simon and his goddamned dog.

The explosion from what seemed almost on top of him was so startling that it knocked him off the stair and sent him tumbling, heels over head, down the flight to the next landing. He lay there for a moment, stunned and bruised as all around him it sounded like the building was under seige.

The windows in the residence building blew out.

All of them, in rapid-fire succession.

One moment they had been glittering in the sunlight, and the next they were raining down toward the square below, millions upon millions of sharp edged fragments. A rain of death.

Chuck staggered, his nose bleeding, but he turned and, even as soldiers shouted and yelled in confusion, he focused all his will on the building just across the compound. He yanked with all his strength and the glass from that other stunning tower shattered as if jet propelled. Then another building, and another—

Soldiers were running, screaming, as glass hurled down on them, deadly hail. There were small chunks and large chunks, uniforms ripped and faces torn. Soldiers went down, flailing and howling, a couple getting it in their eyes.

Everyone was shouting as the glass shower continued. Nobody knew or understood what was happening or where it was coming from. "Extremists!" they were shouting, looking desperately for the enemy, uncomprehending where the threat really was coming from.

Only Quint understood. "It's Simon!" he shouted. "It's Simon! He's doing it!" But he could not be heard above the din.

Chuck staggered and fell and landed on Rommel. The world was whirling around him and it was all he could do to stay conscious. "Get us out of here. . . ." he whispered.

There's glass everywhere. My paws—

Chuck looked around desperately, and spotted at one end of the square a motorcycle and side-car that the MP had been patrolling in. But glass was still falling, crashing all around, and for good measure Chuck looked up, saw the building that Quint's offices were in and yanked out those windows too.

Quint looked up, saw it, and barely covered his head as more glass fell around him. Blood was pouring from hundreds of scratches, and there was glass in his hair, glass everywhere. . . .

Glass worked its way down under his sunglasses and into his right eye. He screamed and fell to the ground, grabbing at it and howling.

Somewhere over the shouts of the other soldiers, he heard an engine rev.

The motorcycle's ignition turned over and it roared toward Chuck and Rommel.

Chuck barely managed to get it to skid to a halt as he stumbled forward and fell headfirst into the sidecar.

Rommel had leaped up on the other side, poised on the wide seat, looking down into the sidecar.

Chuck, nose bleeding profusely now, knew that the falling glass had bought them at most a few moments of surprise. They needed something else, something to buy them extra seconds.

He looked up, saw where Rommel was.

"Turn yourself around," he ordered. "Keep your flank on the seat, put your front paws on the handlebars there."

Rommel did as he was ordered, not understanding. *What's going on?*

"You're driving," snapped Chuck.

He slumped forward in the sidecar so he could see where they were going, and then mentally released the clutch. Compared to the strain of blasting out the glass, that was a picnic.

The vehicle roared forward. Chuck put a small portion of his mind to work holding Rommel securely in place, and the rest of it to the steering.

Soldiers were running everywhere, trying to escape the hail of glass. One of them stumbled, then heard a motorcycle roaring toward them. He looked up and saw a dog was driving it. Chuck Simon was in the sidecar, but the dog was clearly in charge.

If Simon had been driving, the soldier would automatically have shot him. If the soldier had even had a chance

to figure out what was happening, he still might have shot
him. As it was, his mind refused to accept what his eyes
were seeing, and suddenly he was left with no alternative
but to simply leap out of the way as the motorcycle roared
past.

Rommel's ears streamed out behind him. *This isn't bad,*
he said.

"Hold on," said Chuck.

He was ordering the motorcycle to turn, because his
first priority was to get the hell off the glass. The tires
were sturdy, but sooner or later they were going to be
shredded if they didn't get away.

The motorcycle banked left, shot across the square in a
wide U-turn and sped away. From behind them bullets
cracked, and Chuck knew that some soldiers had had the
presence of mind to start shooting at them.

He heard a sound next to him and looked over. A bullet
had thudded into the wall of the sidecar not six inches
away from his leg.

They sped off the concrete square and angled down a
grassy hill, Chuck holding on desperately as it swayed
wildly.

The motorcycle hit the bottom of the hill and leaped
back up onto pavement once more. It skidded out, leaving
a wavering trail of black marks across the paving, and
Chuck nearly lost control. Rommel growled. *Watch it, I
almost fell off,* he snapped.

Chuck ignored him, thinking furiously. They could try
to get over the fence, but the area was too wooded once
they left the main road. They couldn't use the cycle, and
they'd lose valuable time. Besides, for all he knew the
fence was electrified. Coming to a decision, he said "That
way," as much for himself as anything else, and the mo-

torcycle sped off down the road, heading toward the main gate.

Beutel ran out of the building and looked up in amazement. The windows were gone, only a few shards still hanging on to give a reminder of what had once been there.

He ran into the square to see the pandemonium, the officers barking orders into walkie-talkies, everyone shouting at once.

What he did not see was Simon's body lying perforated on the ground. He started to curse profusely, and then saw something that at least made him feel a little better. Quint, screaming, staggering about, with blood pouring out from beneath his sunglasses.

Maybe it hadn't been such a bad day after all.

The soldiers at the front gate were incredulous.

"The *dog* is driving?" one of them said into the walkie-talkie.

The irate voice of their commanding officer shot back at them, "The dog's a front! The man is hiding in the sidecar and he's controlling it. Shoot on sight!"

The two soldiers looked at each other, both silently wondering if someone was having some fun at their expense.

But then, seconds later, they heard the sound of a roaring motorcycle engine. There was a blind curve to the left and that was clearly where it was coming from.

They leaped out of the guard house and, the moment the motorcycle made the turn, they opened fire, spraying a steady stream of ammo at the uncoming cycle.

The cycle kicked back under the barrage and went out of control. It overturned and the gas tank went up. The motorcycle exploded in a burst of flame.

They darted back into the guard house to escape the impact and any stray pieces of flying metal, and one of them barked into the walkie-talkie, "We got 'em! Didn't see the dog, but if the man was hiding in the sidecar, he's dead!"

A furious growl sounded behind them and they turned.

Rommel leaped at them. One of them swung his rifle around and Rommel ignored it, going straight for his throat. The soldier screamed, blood pouring out from between Rommel's jaws, and an instant later the soldier's voice vanished.

The other tried to bring his rifle around, and suddenly he felt himself yanked out of the guard house as if pulled by a huge string.

He tumbled out and fell backward, losing his grip on his rifle. The weapon flew out of his hands and out of reach, clattering to the ground a dozen yards away.

He staggered to his feet and faced Chuck who stood there, arms at his side.

But Chuck was distracted as he screamed into the guard house, "Dammit, Rommel, stop! Stop! I said not to kill him! That wasn't the plan!" The soldier leaped forward, smashing into Chuck and driving him to the ground. He drew his fist back, but Chuck brought up his knee and flipped the soldier back over his head. As he did so, he held onto the soldier's right hand and when the soldier landed on his chest, Chuck was already on his back and holding his right arm around and behind him. The soldier screamed, thinking the arm was going to be torn out of its socket.

"I'm really, really sorry about this," said Chuck, as he picked up a rock and brought it down on the back of the soldier's head.

* * *

The reinforcements finally arrived, still cut up and bleeding from all the glass.

They found one dead soldier, his throat torn out, and another soldier unconscious and in his underwear. The front gate was wide open.

"Well, Corporal Marsh," said the ticket seller a little nervously, glancing at the large dog next to the soldier, "normally we don't allow such animals on the bus unless they're seeing-eye dogs. . . ."

"He's specially trained," said Chuck, chafing a little in the uniform that was just a shade too small for him. "K-9 Corps. He won't hurt a flea, unless I order him to."

"If you'll vouch for him—"

"Absolutely, yes."

Moments later they had purchased a ticket and were walking down the line of people. Chuck casually scanned the impressions of the people as he passed by and stopped at one young man. "You going to Detroit?" he asked.

The young man nodded, looking confused.

"Here," said Chuck, handing the young man the ticket he'd just purchased. "I was going to Detroit, but I just got word all leaves were cancelled. Gotta get back to my post. Save you a wait on line."

The young man said, "But you'll be out the money—"

"Just the government's money. They were sending me. You just got yourself a free ride."

"Well . . . thanks," said the young man, barely able to believe his good fortune.

Chuck then went outside to the parking lot, found a car that he liked, mentally unlocked the door and, within moments, had manipulated the ignition. The car roared to life.

He glanced through the glove compartment and found

some ID in it. As soon as he didn't need the car anymore he would contact the owner and inform them of where the car could be found.

He backed out and turned onto the street.

Rommel lay next to him on the seat and Chuck, still angry from earlier, said, "You weren't supposed to kill him. The motorcycle was to distract them while we came around from the woods. I don't want any more blood on my hands, you understand?"

They'd have killed you if they had the chance.

"Killing is wrong," said Chuck firmly.

It's more wrong if they kill you than if you kill them.

"If anyone kills, it's wrong."

When do we eat?

"Later," sighed Chuck.

He passed signs for the entrance ramp onto the highway and turned onto it.

Sooner or later, and probably much sooner than later, the Complex would find that Marsh's Card had been used to purchase that bus ticket. The poor people on that Detroit-bound bus were going to find themselves pulled over at some point by a small army battalion and searched, causing all kinds of fear and confusion.

Wrecking other people's plans. Stealing and misusing ID. Stealing a car. Shattering windows and attacking soldiers. Traveling with an animal ready to kill in his name. And he himself had killed in unbridled fury.

He realized that, with every one of his actions, he increased the chances that much more that he was probably going straight to hell.

Well, considering that that was what he felt like he was running away from, there was something bleakly symmetrical about it all.

October 13, 2021

18

GWYNN, SOMETIMES KNOWN as Penguin, the owner and operator of the Four Star Carnival and Circus, was awakened from his slumber shortly after midnight by a pounding at the door. He sat up in irritation, reached for his glasses in the darkness, and rolled out of bed. Waddling over to the door of his private Winnebago (the only man in the circus to have that particular perk), Gwynn threw the door open and snarled, "This better be important."

Men in dark suits stood outside, blending in with the night. Gwynn couldn't see how many there were, but there looked to be about ten of them.

The one who had been knocking on the door had a strange, almost demented smile that sent chills through Gwynn.

"My name is Beutel," he said softly. "We—my associates and I—are looking for a gentleman that we understand is in your employ."

"Is that a fact?"

"Yes, sir," said Beutel, all politeness. "We'd appreciate your cooperation." He held up ID. "We're with the Complex."

Gwynn snorted. "I don't care if you're with Ringling

Brothers. You're not coming in here in the middle of a night to roust one of my people."

"It's for your own safety, sir. The man we're looking for is wanted for murder. His name is Charles Anthony Simon," and he held up a small photograph. "Have you seen him?"

Gwynn blinked, staring at the picture. He recognized it instantly.

"No," was his prompt response.

Beutel stared at him for a long moment. He still appeared very friendly. "Mr. Gwynn," he said scoldingly, "I think you're fibbing. Now I know you're being loyal because Mr. Simon was responsible for saving one of your people who was hospitalized yesterday. That was very brave of him. It's admirable to support someone who has done you a good turn. But it's necessary that you cooperate with us, Mr. Gwynn."

"Yeah? Why's that?"

There was the sound of several hammers being drawn back, and several guns were now aimed directly at Gwynn. Beutel, whose hands were at his sides, spread them apologetically.

"Because otherwise we'll have to blow your fucking brains out," said Beutel.

Within fifteen minutes the entire population of the circus was milling about in confusion. Gwynn was trying to elicit information, but from everyone the answer was the same. No one had seen Chuck.

Dakota stood off to the side, wearing a football jersey that came to about mid-thigh. Her arms were folded, her hair down. She watched the proceedings with distaste, and raised an eyebrow as the one who'd been identified as Beutel came toward her. He stopped several feet away and studied her.

"You were friendly with Chuck Simon," he said.

"Was that his last name?" she replied calmly. "Around here we're pretty much on a first name basis. We don't generally worry about unnecessary information."

"Weeellllll," said Beutel in that protracted way he had, "I wouldn't think of it as particularly unnecessary right now. Anything we can find out about Chuck Simon will be of help."

"If you're so all-fired certain he's here, why don't you just look around."

"He was here," said Beutel with certainty. "He's not now."

Dakota had seen Chuck speak with the same kind of confidence that this man now displayed. There was no guesswork, there was simply knowledge. Knowledge about things that shouldn't be easily known, or even possibly known.

Where was Chuck, anyway? She'd seen him a while ago, shortly before midnight, it seemed. He'd been walking across the quiet circus grounds, that monster of a dog nearby him. . . .

Had he been carrying something? A shoulder bag, or backpack? She wasn't sure now. She thought he might have been . . .

That son of a bitch. He'd left. Left without saying goodbye. Her heart sank just a bit. She had really, really wanted to reward him, in her own inimitable style, for the way that he had rescued Harry from the lions. But for the hours after that he had seemed distant and distracted, and she was willing to wait a day or so until the fright and shock of the encounter had worn off. But he had vanished.

Definitely annoying.

Beutel stared at her silently for a time longer and then turned and spoke in a loud voice. "People," he called out, "you don't seem to realize the gravity of the situation. We want you to cooperate."

From somewhere in the darkness, one of the circus people called out, "Fuck you."

Beutel raised an eyebrow and looked over the large group, bathed in the flood lights rigged on poles overhead. "Do I take that to be a group consensus? Mr. Gwynn?"

Gwynn stood there, feeling the eyes of all his people on him.

This man, these men, had come out of the darkness, flashing their identifications with the red logos, waving their weapons, threatening. They were acting far more like murderers than the man they were hunting. The man who had risked his life to save the lion tamer.

"Yes," said Gwynn tightly. "That's the consensus. Even if Chuck were here, we wouldn't turn him over."

"All right," said Beutel, and shot Gwynn.

Beutel didn't use guns often, but they frequently made a superb impact on watchers. He smiled as Gwynn fell back, screaming, blood fountaining from his leg. The others stood there, paralyzed.

"Is there anyone who wishes to be the new spokesman?" asked Beutel. He pointed the gun at Dakota. "How about yourself?"

Dakota stood there, arms still folded, her eyes smoldering.

"Now, ma'am, don't do this to yourself," Beutel warned her.

The air seemed to congeal around Dakota and suddenly blew her forward. She stumbled and fell, hitting the ground in front of Beutel, her football jersey falling to around her hips.

"Make yourself decent, please," Beutel said scoldingly.

He grabbed her and yanked her to her feet, holding the gun on her. "Congratulations," he said softly. "You are now the new spokeswoman for this group. Now . . . do you speak for all of them in saying that you are not going to cooperate?"

Gwynn writhed on the ground, moaning, trying to stanch the bleeding.

"I warn you," said Beutel, putting the gun to Dakota's head.

"You bastard," and now Dexter and Paul were starting to advance on him. The other dark men got in the way, and the whole crowd was starting to surge forward.

Beutel turned and tossed off a shot, striking Dexter in the shoulder. He went down and the others froze as well.

"You don't know who you're screwing with!" shouted Beutel. "I'm going easy on you people. But if somebody—"

He froze. Then he turned to the other men. "He's here. I knew it." He turned toward Dakota and smiled. "I knew if I created enough of a ruckus, he'd sense it and come back. The sap."

He swung his hand back and smacked her across the jaw, sending her to the ground. "Spread out!" he shouted. "Find him! He's here somewhere, but I can't pinpoint him. Torelli, Koch, keep the weapons on the fun factory here." He pointed at the circus people, and the two agents who had been named stood in front of the crowd with AK-74s aimed at them, capable of turning the people into hamburger if they had to.

"Stay in twos!" shouted Beutel. "If you find him, summon me."

Suddenly a wall of the great tent ripped down on its own.

Beutel, and the cluster of men around him, spun at the sound.

They found themselves looking down the muzzle of a cannon, the one used for the human cannonball act.

"Scatter!" shouted Beutel, sending out a TK blast to try and alter the aim of the cannon.

Too slow, too late. The cannon exploded, discharging its contents.

Straw and horse manure.

Chuck had gone straight to the stables and, using his TK, had sent the contents of the stables hurtling into the cannon. Then he'd lit the sucker, aimed, psychically torn down the tent side and let fly.

It came with too much force and impact for even Beutel to slow down. The agents, including the ones with the automatic weapons, were bowled over by the blast, and when they staggered to their feet they were covered with the contents. Several were already mercifully unconscious.

"Get him!" screamed Beutel, and he started toward the circus tent.

And then Dakota, suddenly realizing that no one was covering them, screamed out, at the top of her lungs, *"HEY, RUBE!"*

Responding to the age-old carny cry for help, the circus performers charged forward. The agents, already moving clumsily and stinking of horseshit, went down in the first wave, pummeled to the ground. A couple managed to get off a shot or two, but they were all misses.

Beutel ripped off his jacket and hurled it to the ground. "You idiots!" he shouted. He gestured, and the performers who were charging him were hurled back as if yanked by invisible strings. He spun and charged toward the tent, leaping in through the ripped down wall.

Dakota and two others followed him in. Nearby were the props for Paul's hatchet-throwing act, embedded in an upright wooden board with the outline of a female drawn on it. Beutel glanced at it and the hatchets ripped free, turned and went spinning toward the circus performers.

Dakota screamed and the three of them tried to back up, but the hatchets were circling them now, spinning in a vicious line of death.

"Psi-Man!" he shouted. "Show yourself! And keep that damned dog out of it, y'hear? This is between you and me! Show yourself or they die! Psi-Man!"

Chuck came out from behind the bleachers and stepped into the center ring. "Here, Beutel," he called out. "I'm over here."

Beutel smiled.

"Let them go, Beutel," snapped Chuck. "They're not a part of this."

The hatchets dropped to the ground.

The moment they did, Chuck shouted "Get out of here, all of you! I mean it! I can handle this!"

"Oh, can you?" said Beutel slowly, approaching Chuck. He was smiling, his fingers twitching. "Quint is very anxious to see you . . . at least, see you as best he can. He's wearing an eyepatch these days. That's another one you can chalk up for yourself."

"Go back to Quint," said Chuck, "and tell him that I'm never going back. I'll never be what you want me to be."

"That all depends," said Beutel pleasantly. "Quint still wants you to be an assassin. I just want you to be dead."

A rope that was to Chuck's right suddenly lashed up at him, wrapping itself around him, pinioning his arms. He staggered as, before he could move, the rope snared around his throat.

"This is how Jeffries bought it," Beutel told him.

Chuck fought off the panic, concentrated on prying the rope from around his throat. Beutel closed on him and Chuck suddenly dropped to the ground. His legs lashed out, snaring Beutel behind the knees and knocking him flat.

The fall disrupted Beutel's concentration and the ropes slackened. Chuck immediately shook them off and Beutel, furious, brought the air molecules around Chuck to life. A furious wind buffeted Chuck back and he staggered and stumbled over the edge of the uprised ring.

From the darkness, Rommel barked furiously and Beutel froze, the blood draining from his face.

"No, Rommel, stay!" shouted Chuck. And he leaped straight toward Beutel, aided by the thrust of his TK power. He plowed into Beutel, knocking him back. Beutel tried to mentally force him off, but Chuck's power blocked his own, and Chuck grabbed his wrist and twisted Beutel around. Beutel shrieked, his arm pulling against the joint, and Chuck smashed him headfirst into a nearby trapeze pole.

Dazed, Beutel reached out toward the hatchets. They rose up and hurtled toward Chuck.

Chuck swung his torso to the right and left, brushing the hatchets aside with sweeps of his forearm. But the distraction was enough for Beutel to recover and suddenly a blast of pure TK power lifted Chuck up and sent him hurtling toward the top of the circus tent.

The ground spun out beneath him and then, several hundred feet in the air, the blast depleted itself and he started to fall. The ground came at him with dizzying speed, and somewhere in the distance he heard Beutel laughing loudly.

Chuck blasted out at the ground, trying to slow his fall. With the velocity of his descent added in, his poundage increased tremendously. The world started to gray out in front of him, and he reached out desperately, slowed down a bit but nowhere near enough to save himself.

His hand hit a wire and his fist closed around it. He brought the other hand around, and when he opened his eyes he saw he was dangling from the highwire.

He looked down. No net.

The ground seemed to turn under him. It was a rotten time to discover that heights made him edgy. Then again, dangling from a tightrope would make anyone untrained edgy. Chuck gulped, unable to get the image of the fall from his mind.

Beutel looked up, laughing hysterically at Chuck's danger. Quickly he ran through all the ways he could possibly send Chuck plummeting to his death, and so wasn't paying attention when the large hatchet slammed into his head.

He fell to the ground, barely breathing, and Dakota stood behind him, the hatchet clutched in her hand, wishing like hell she'd had the nerve to use the blade edge instead of the back. She'd only creased his skull instead of cutting it open. "Chuck!" she shouted. "Hold on!"

She ran up and scrambled up the ladder that led to the platform. Within seconds she was there and, dangling helplessly, so was Chuck. "Okay now, make your way over."

"I'm not gonna make it!" he shouted.

"Sure you are. It's easy." For once, she was the one who felt totally in control.

With utter confidence she walked out onto the tightrope, balancing assuredly. "You're going to be fine," she said. "You and your pal . . . you got some act there. But it can't begin to touch mine."

Within seconds she was there and she crouched down. "Now come on," she said. "Don't look down."

Naturally he looked down. He toyed with the idea that perhaps he could somehow lower himself to the ground. But he couldn't bring himself to simply let go and trust his power to accomplish that.

"Come on. Start making your way over." She backed up. "One hand over the other. Come on. I'm right here."

He started to slide his hand over.

"That's it," she said. "That's right."

From below him a growl caught his attention. Rommel was starting to come out of the shadow and advance on Beutel.

With all his power he shouted "No, Rommel! Leave him alone! Back off!"

The dog staggered under the mental assault over their connection.

Beutel woke up. He saw the dog, not ten paces away, saw Chuck still hundreds of feet above the ground. Saw the bitch in the football jersey.

He sent out a bolt of force at the end of the tightrope and it snapped free of its moorings.

Dakota screamed as the rope suddenly went slack under her and she tumbled off. Chuck, still gripping with one hand, lashed out and snagged her around the waist, but now the two of them were falling.

They swung through the air, cutting a dazzling arc, heading for the pole that the tightrope was moored to at the other end. And this time, terrified not only for himself but for Dakota, Chuck slowed down the speed of their swing. Nevertheless they smashed into the far pole with horrifying speed. Chuck never let go of the rope, and took the brunt of the impact. It stunned him and his grasp came free, but now Dakota was holding on, the other arm supporting Chuck. They dangled there, now only about a hundred feet off the ground.

Rommel, freed of Chuck's control, leaped at Beutel.

Beutel saw him coming and howled in fear and terror, unable to focus his TK power as Rommel bore down on him. He grabbed out at the only thing nearby, the hatchet. He swung it up and around just as Rommel leaped and slammed the hatchet into Rommel's front shoulder.

Rommel let out a deafening roar and tumbled away. The hatchet fell to the ground and Rommel spun, blood staining his fur.

Beutel got to his feet and grabbed up the hatchet, heart pounding against his chest, his legs trembling. Rommel opened wide his jaws, bellowed defiance, and leaped at him. Beutel swung the hatchet and missed and Rommel's jaws clamped down on the arm as it completed its downswing. His jaws snapped shut and through and as a screaming Beutel tried to pull away, Rommel's jaws slid down the forearm, shredding skin, muscle and tissue.

Beutel yanked the arm away, fell to the ground, felt warmth covering him, blood pouring from his wrist. His wrist—

—his hand was gone.

He looked up in nauseated horror and saw Rommel spit out the fist. Rommel growled and took a step toward him on unsteady legs, and then the great dog fell over, the stain on his fur widening.

Beutel staggered to his feet and Rommel growled at him, snapping his jaws.

The agent ran. He grabbed up his jacket as he dashed out of the tent and wrapped it around his arm. The jacket promptly became soaked with blood.

He saw his team unconscious and in the process of being tied up. He tried not to pass out as a wave of nausea swept over him. He turned and ran, ran toward woods that lay nearby, and the darkness of the trees swallowed him up.

Roustabouts were running into the tent, and they saw Dakota, clutching desperately onto a barely conscious Chuck. Immediately they were swarming up and around her, shimmying the poles and going up the ladder. Within moments they were safely on the ground.

"The dog!" cried out Dakota. "Take care of the dog! He's hurt."

Several men went to the dog, and one of them, the horse trainer, a man named Taylor, immediately called out for wet cloths and bandages.

As they worked on Rommel, Chuck slowly started to come around. He blinked, his head in Dakota's lap. "What happened?" he asked.

"Mad night of passion," she told him. "The earth moved. Was it good for you too?"

He sat upright and suddenly shouted "Rommel!" He ran to the dog's side, leaving Dakota there with her hands on her hips.

"That's it," she said. "When a man runs away from my lap to be with a dog, it's time to become a nun."

Chuck looked fearfully at the ugly wound in Rommel's shoulder. Taylor looked up and said, "You're lucky. Couple inches higher, could've taken off the dog's head."

Far in the distance an ambulance was coming, and there were police sirens.

Rommel looked up at Chuck. *You're going to get me killed with this attitude of yours.*

Chuck sighed. "We'll discuss it later."

The men surrounding them looked from one to the other and didn't ask who Chuck was talking to.

"Can he walk?" said Chuck.

Of course I can walk.

"I don't think so," said Taylor.

With what sounded very much like a human grunt of disgust, Rommel staggered to his feet.

"We've gotta get out of here," said Chuck.

"Cops are coming," observed Taylor. "They'll have lots of questions about those men . . . and you."

"That's why."

Dakota had come up behind them. "Taylor, bring the pick-up truck around."

"Penguin'll be mad," said Taylor. "He doesn't like to fuck with the police, and they'll want to know—"

"Screw Penguin," said Dakota. "Bring the goddamn pick-up around."

Another one of the men ran up to do as she said.

By the time the cops got there, Dakota, Chuck, and Rommel were gone.

19

As THE GRAY sky was highlighted by the rising sun, somewhere unseen behind the clouds, the pick-up truck bounced noisily down the road.

I don't like this at all, grumbled Rommel from the rear.

In the cab of the truck, Chuck replied, "Tolerate it the best you can. I'm sorry you're uncomfortable."

Dakota, who was driving, glanced at Chuck. "You're talking to the dog, aren't you."

Why fight it, he wondered. "Yes, I'm talking to the dog."

"Dog talking back?"

"Uh huh."

"Somehow that doesn't surprise me."

She was silent for a time and then she said, "I'm thinking of quitting the circus. Care to have someone tag along?"

He looked at her disbelieving. "I don't think so," he said. "Just drop us a couple miles up and we can thumb a ride from there."

"Why can't I come?"

"It's kind of dangerous, Dakota."

"So's walking a tightrope."

I'm hungry. And I want to kill the next ones who try to kill us.

Chuck sighed. "We'll discuss it."

"We will?" said Dakota.

"I wasn't talking to you," he said. "I was talking to the dog."

"Oh," she said. "That old ploy."

The pick-up truck rolled down the highway and the sun still refused to shine.